As they sat on a blanket under a copse of pine trees, Martie's eyes sparkled wickedly. "You know, this would be a wonderful place to make love," she said provocatively.

Paul choked on his fried chicken. What was she up to now? he wondered. He could see the imp in her expression and decided to keep silent, let her lead the way.

"Once down in Tijuana I did the fandango on top of Rafael's bar. I was dancing so hard my earrings fell into the guacamole, and later everyone drank champagne from my slipper."

He still said nothing.

"Aren't you shocked?" she asked.

"Am I supposed to be?" he answered.

This wasn't at all how she'd planned it. He was supposed to see how unsuitable she was and walk off in disgust. "Don't you even want to know who Rafael is?"

"If you want to tell me."

"He's a bullfighter who taught me to drive fast cars and gamble."

"Do you want me to pass judgment? If so, I'm afraid I'll have to disappoint you."

She pouted for a moment, then accepted her failure to dismay him.

"You know," he said then, "you were right about this place."

Martie had a sudden vision of them writhing in ecstasy on the carpet of pine needles, and she jumped up. If she didn't put a city block between them quickly, she couldn't be held responsible for what she did.

Paul's hand snaked out and caught her wrist. Pulling her down beside him, he commanded quietly, "Stay. . . ."

WHAT ARE *LOVESWEPT* ROMANCES?

They are stories of true romance and touching emotion. We believe those two very important ingredients are constants in our highly sensual and very believable stories in the *LOVESWEPT* line. Our goal is to give you, the reader, stories of consistently high quality that may sometimes make you laugh, sometimes make you cry, but are always fresh and creative and contain many delightful surprises within their pages.

Most romance fans read an enormous number of books. Those they truly love, they keep. Others may be traded with friends and soon forgotten. We hope that each *LOVESWEPT* romance will be a treasure—a "keeper." We will always try to publish

LOVE STORIES YOU'LL NEVER FORGET
BY AUTHORS YOU'LL ALWAYS REMEMBER

The Editors

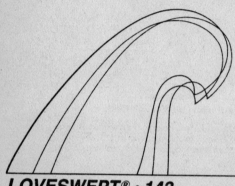

LOVESWEPT® • 143
Peggy Webb
Donovan's Angel

BANTAM BOOKS
TORONTO • NEW YORK • LONDON • SYDNEY • AUCKLAND

DONOVAN'S ANGEL

A Bantam Book / June 1986

LOVESWEPT® *and the wave device are trademarks
of Bantam Books, Inc. Registered in U.S. Patent
and Trademark Office and elsewhere.*

ISBN 0-553-21760-7

Published simultaneously in the United States and Canada

---

*Bantam Books are published by Bantam Books, Inc. Its
trademark, consisting of the words "Bantam Books" and
the portrayal of a rooster, is Registered in U.S. Patent and
Trademark Office and in other countries. Marca Registrada.
Bantam Books, Inc., 666 Fifth Avenue, New York, New
York 10103.*

PRINTED IN THE UNITED STATES OF AMERICA

O   0 9 8 7 6 5 4 3 2 1

For the real Baby,
who inspired the book

One

The crisp, dry leaves rattled like old bones as Martie swung her rake briskly back and forth. She sang as she worked, lifting her lusty contralto voice in joyful abandon. Nearby, a large blue-gray Siamese cat gingerly tested the growing pile of leaves with a delicate paw.

Plop! A tattered marigold landed at Martie's feet. "Why, thank you, Baby." Dropping the rake, she knelt beside her gangly-legged golden retriever puppy and playfully scratched the soft, pale fur under her neck. "Where have you been this morning?"

Baby's tail thumped the ground as she bathed her adored owner's hand with a wet, pink tongue.

Giving her puppy one last pat, Martie picked up the drooping yellow flower and stuck it behind her ear. Baby pranced happily around the yard, stopping long enough to give the cat a thrill by nipping at his tail, and then she disappeared through a gap in the tall clapboard fence.

Martie finished raking and sat beside an unkempt flower bed to attack the weeds that had established residence there. She reveled in the feel of the black, loamy earth under her hands. Her patch of earth, she thought. Her house. Her town. It felt wonderful to belong someplace, and she was glad all over that she had chosen this little town to settle down in after all her vagabond years. The minute she'd seen Pontotoc she had known that this was a good place to hang her hat. There was a feeling of permanence about it, a solid sense that generations had sat under its ancient oak trees and that countless others would come along to enjoy the splendid rapport between civilization and nature in this sleepy Southern town.

Absorbed in her work and her thoughts, Martie was completely unaware of the growing pile of marigolds behind her. Marigolds without leaves, marigolds with roots, marigolds with tattered heads, homeless marigolds gasping for breath in the jaws of Baby. As Martie turned to reach for a trowel, she saw the mountain of wilting flowers and the golden wave of Baby's tail as she disappeared through a hole in the fence.

"Good grief! What have you done?" she cried, clutching a mutilated marigold. "Come back here!" The dog blissfully ignored the command.

The quickest way to see what her rambunctious pet was up to, she decided, was to climb the oak tree, jump down on the other side of the fence, and follow her. She just hoped an irate gardener with a gun wasn't waiting on the other side. Knotting her bright peasant skirt between her legs, she grabbed a low-hanging branch and swung up the tree. Quickly she shinned up the trunk, her legs navigating the limbs with ease. Branches snatched at her topknot of white-gold hair, pulling random curls down around her neck and forehead. She straddled a fat limb and inched along until she was on the other side of the fence. Parting the leaves, she peered down into total devastation. A once proud flower bed was almost naked, and her pet was digging with a vengeance, determined to strip the bed of its few remaining flowers.

"No, Baby," she called sharply.

Doleful brown eyes lifted up to the sound of a familiar voice. There was a moment's pause as clouds of dust settled to the ground; then, reluctantly, Baby stopped digging and scampered back through the fence.

Martie judged the distance to the ground. It was time to face the music. Maybe she would get lucky. Maybe the owner of this flower bed was allergic to marigolds and had been planning to have them dug up anyway. She looked at the ground again. The fence was taller than she had imagined, and the tree trunk was on the other side. She would have to swing down from the limb, Tarzan style. Of course she had done more daring things in her lifetime, but she was partial to her bones. She didn't relish the idea of breaking them for the sake of a few flowers.

The bark scraped her knee as she shifted her legs and dangled from the limb. She lost her precarious grip, and the upturned earth met her body with a soft *whump!* With her face in the dirt and her rump saluting the breeze, she wriggled experimentally. Thank goodness, nothing seemed to be broken.

"Well, hello there."

The resonant tones of that voice vibrated all the way down to her toes. She twisted her upended bottom so fast that she made lightning look slow. Underneath the smudges, her face was bright pink.

"Hi," she said as she looked up into the face of a very large man. He had a pair of silver-gray eyes that were startlingly light in the deep tan of his face, and a lock of black hair hung down over his forehead as if mussed by the careless hand of a loving wife. Martie felt a quick flash of irritation at the loving wife, and the unexpected thought muddled her usually sharp mind. "I'm planting flowers." Her hands sifted aimlessly through the dirt.

"I beg your pardon." His lips curved upward into the most remarkable smile she had ever seen. Sunshine and rainbows and Christmas-morning joy all seemed to be wrapped up in that smile.

Her violet eyes widened a fraction as she met that disconcerting smile. Reluctantly she tore her eyes away from the mobile mouth and focused her attention on his chin. It was square and steady, with a cleft on its beard-shadowed surface. A small puff of wind whispered through the red-gold leaves of the tree and playfully lifted the gleaming tendrils of hair off her forehead as she sat silently, acknowledging the presence of the man standing above her. Theirs was a meeting as ancient as time, a primitive recognition of the magic that flows between man and woman.

As the knowledge surged through her, her confidence returned. "I'm Martie Fleming, your new backyard neighbor."

"I'm Paul Donovan." He couldn't tear his eyes away from the Botticelli-angel face. It was the first time in his thirty-five years that he'd felt tongue-tied. There must be something that he needed to say, but all he could think of was bending down to wipe the smudge from her suntanned cheek. Instead, he extended his hand. "Here," he said. "Let me help you up." If he thought it was strange that a woman had fallen from the sky into his flower bed, he didn't say so. He was too busy counting his blessings.

Martie took his hand and sprang lightly to her feet. "I came to apologize about your flowers. My dog decided to do some fall gardening. I'm afraid that all your marigolds are in a dying heap in my backyard."

He decided that her voice was like music. Angel music. She could have told him that his blue jeans were on fire and he wouldn't have moved a muscle. He was too entranced by the vision that had dropped into his life. "I was never partial to marigolds."

"What a relief. I expected at least twenty lashes."

"Apparently so did your dog. Where is he?"

"He's a she. A four-month-old golden retriever *puppy* who has her lovable moments. Today is not one of them." She scanned the immaculate yard. "She never hangs around when she knows justice is at hand."

Paul's smile widened. He couldn't imagine her meting out justice. She seemed so much more at home with laughter. Gray eyes met violet, and the Indian-summer day took on a golden hue. Martie forgot about the marigolds, and he forgot that he had come outside to get his socks off the clothes-line.

"I'm glad you did," he said.

"Did what?"

"Hang around."

"For my punishment?" She had a generous smile, a perfect showcase for teeth that were even and as white as pearls. Paul decided that everything about her was perfect. Even the dirt on her face suited the gamine he saw peering out of her remarkable eyes. Such eyes! As if God had mixed a bit of sky with dark purple flowers and thrown in a dash of sunshine for good measure.

"No, for a cup of tea."

Martie swiped the dirt on her cheek and smeared it behind her ear. "It's the best I can do on such short notice." The pixie smile flashed again. "And I do adore get-acquainted parties. Do you have lots of sugar? If we're going to make this a neighborly tradition—sharing tea—I have to warn you that I consume more sugar than a honey bear."

Paul loved the way she talked with her whole body. Rows of plastic bracelets jangled on her arm, her long dangle earrings swayed with the motion of her head, and the ruffles on her off-the-shoulder blouse floated around her, punctuating her phrases. Somehow it seemed perfectly natural to him that she would wear such a flamboyant outfit to climb a tree. "I'll remember that," he replied.

The screeching of tires shattered their magic world, and they focused their attention on the impressively large woman emerging from an antique baby-blue Cadillac. "Yoo-hoo!" she called. Her voice was only twice as loud as the orange flowers on her tent dress. The slamming of her car door resounded in the still October day, and she rolled toward them with the purposefulness of an army tank. "I have to talk . . ." She stopped in mid-sentence as she became aware of the silver-blond haired woman standing in the ruined flower bed. As her eyes roamed over the dirty face, the flashy jewelry, and the skirt, brazenly tied between the woman's bare legs, Miss Beulah Grady's nose seemed to rearrange itself on her face. "I wasn't aware that you had company." Coming from her pursed lips, "company" sounded like the biggest scourge since the bubonic plague.

Unaware of the hurricane brewing behind Miss Beulah's tight face, Paul made the introductions. "We were just going inside for a cup of tea, Miss Beulah. Won't you join us?"

"As a matter of fact, a spot of tea might help. I didn't sleep a wink last night for thinking about the disaster that has struck our little community. It's a sin and disgrace. A dis-*grace.*" She billowed along behind Paul and Martie, talking every breath. The screen door banged shut behind her as they entered a high-ceilinged parlor. Miss Beulah Grady settled into an overstuffed chair with sagging springs and propped her hands on her fat knees. And continued to talk.

"You two make yourselves at home while I get the tea." Paul winked at Martie. He had no qualms whatsoever about leaving her with Pontotoc's self-appointed watchdog of morality. Anybody who could fall out of a tree and handle herself with such aplomb would be safe with Attila the Hun. He whistled as he worked. Life was full of wonderful surprises, he reflected. And today's surprise had come in a package that fairly took his breath away.

Martie only half listened to Miss Beulah's chatter as she studied the parlor. Odds and ends of furniture that looked as if they had recently come from somebody's attic were scattered around the large room. A brand-new sofa occupied the center of the room, its unsullied brightness making everything else seem faded. She smiled. Whatever else his vices were, it couldn't be said of Paul Donovan that he craved material possessions. Oh, she liked the man. She liked him immensely.

Miss Beulah interrupted her thoughts. "What do you do, Miss Fleming? You never did say."

"What do I do about what, Miss Grady?" Martie didn't know why she said that. On occasion her impish sense of humor had caused her friends to call her perverse. She leaned back in her chair and noticed that her skirt was still knotted between her legs. She might as well leave it, she decided. As a matter of fact, she kind of liked it that way.

"For a *living*." Miss Beulah had a habit of emphasizing words when she was riled. And there was no doubt about it: the woman sitting in the parlor riled her considerably.

"I teach. . . ."

"You don't look like any teacher I ever saw . . . that funny-colored hair and all. I was telling Essie Mae the other day . . . Essie Mae, I said, what's this world coming to when a woman can go down to the drugstore and buy her hair color in a bottle?"

"My hair is natural."

"You sure could have fooled me. And those *clothes*. I never saw any teacher wearing such a getup as that."

"I wasn't teaching today. I was working in my yard."

"You do yard work in that . . . that *gypsy* skirt?"

"Of course. I'm not bound by convention. I wear whatever suits my mood." She glanced up as Paul entered the room. He had overheard her last remark, and his eyes were crinkled at the corners and twinkling with mirth. Martie flashed a radiant smile in his direction and wished she had fallen out of his tree sooner.

"Here you are, Miss Beulah. With a twist of lemon, just the way you like it." Then he turned to Martie. His hand touched hers as he gave her the chipped china teacup. "And lots of sugar for you, Martie."

She wanted to grab his sun-warmed hand and hang on. It was electric, dynamite. This man pulsed with energy and strength. And that voice! It made her want to stand up and cheer. She wondered if he were a singer.

Miss Beulah ignored her tea and focused on Paul. "I'm so glad you're back, Reverend. . . ."

"Damn!" Martie's back stiffened as the shocked whisper echoed in the room.

"Did you say something, Miss Fleming?" Miss Beulah lifted her eyebrows until they disappeared into her Mamie Eisenhower bangs.

"I said, damask. This chair is covered with rose damask." Oh, damn the luck, anyway, she thought, taking a big gulp of her tea. A preacher! Stuffed shirts and stiff upper lips and going by the book and whatever happened to the carousel? Living in a fishbowl and being oh-so-correct and whatever happened to swimming naked in the moonlight? If she had been home, she would have kicked something. Instead, she lowered her eyes to her teacup and said good-bye to an improbable relationship before it had ever begun.

Paul watched all these emotions cross her face. He had half expected her reaction, but he was not prepared for the intensity of his own feelings. Why was she shutting him out without taking the time to know the man behind the profession? he wondered. Why was she throwing away magic—and he knew that together they would be magic—without a second thought? He would make her see him as a man. He had to.

"Aren't you curious about what's underneath the covering, Martie?" he asked gently.

She felt as if all the breath had been knocked out of her. The minister wasn't talking about chairs. And that made him all the more dangerous. "Not in the least," she lied.

"Your actions belie your words. A woman who climbs a tree to see what's on the other side of the fence exhibits a great deal of curiosity."

"I thought we were talking about chairs. How did fences get into this conversation?" Miss Beulah might as well have been a knot on the wall for all the attention she received. Paul and Martie were absorbed in one another, cut off entirely from the rest of the world. Even the furniture had faded into nothingness.

"Evasive tactics won't work, Martie. Tenacity is my strong point."

"And stubbornness is mine."

Miss Beulah Grady was completely unaware that she had witnessed a preliminary skirmish. Her eyes were shut to the lifting of the shield and the counterthrust of the sword. She didn't smell the smoke or hear the battle cry. If she had, she would have run like hell. Instead, she stepped right into the fray. "As I was saying, Reverend, I have the gravest matter to report to you. One of absolutely *cataclysmic* proportions."

"I'm always here to listen to the problems of my parishioners." Paul made the transition so smoothly that Martie almost believed she had dreamed their exchange. She thought of slipping quietly out the door, but discretion was not her style. It would be much more fun to go out with a drumroll and a trumpet fanfare. All she had to do was wait for the band to march by. She didn't have long to wait.

"I don't know if you are aware of this, Reverend, but there is a honky-tonk in this neighborhood." Hot on the trail of scandalous doings, Miss Beulah was in her element. Perspiration beaded her upper lip, and her hands trembled when she talked.

"Are you certain, Miss Beulah? I've heard of no such establishment."

"Am I *certain*? Why, Reverend Donovan, that sleazy music well-nigh blew me out of my bed last night. I never heard such whumping and pounding in all my life! For a minute there I thought it was Satan and his band marching through Pontotoc. Or at least the Russians."

Paul tried unsuccessfully to hide his smile behind his teacup, and Martie's sides were shaking with laughter. She thought this was almost as much fun as falling over the fence.

Miss Beulah took a gulping breath and continued her tirade. The orange flowers on her dress heaved up and down. "I'm telling you . . . something has to be done. It's a sin and disgrace. A disgrace. And right behind the parsonage, too. Just beyond that cyclone fence."

Martie met Paul's gaze over the teacup. For a moment laughter bubbled up inside as she started to explain what was going on behind the cyclone fence. Then she thought she saw a question in his eyes. Well, damn it all, let them think she ran a honky-tonk, she decided. It was probably the quickest way in the world to put an end to the music she had been hearing ever since she'd met the man with the quicksilver eyes.

Her cup rattled against the saucer as she plopped it down on a scarred end table. "I own that honky-tonk behind the cyclone fence." She glared defiantly at Paul. *Now* let him smile and talk about neighborly cups of tea and curiosity and fences and things that made her heart go bump!

"I should have known," Miss Beulah blurted out.

Paul spoke quietly. "Just a moment, Miss Beulah." Why was she doing this? he wondered. Women who adored golden retrievers and wore tattered marigolds behind their ears didn't operate beer joints. "As a matter of fact, I heard the music myself. I thought it was rather lively and joyful-sounding. I'm sure Martie is playing a joke on us." He looked directly into her eyes. "Aren't you?"

The question burned through her, singeing her heart, and she almost told him the truth. Almost. "Why should I deny it? Miss Beulah heard the music. So did you." She turned to Miss Beulah. "And by the way, it's not sleazy music. I call it jazzy juba juke music." She bounced out of her chair.

"It's the kind of music that adds pizazz to life. Good day, all." She flounced out of the room with a brilliant demonstration of pizazz.

"Martie, wait." Paul's entreaty fell on deaf ears.

"Well, I *never*." Miss Beulah fanned herself with her fat hands. "It just makes my blood boil. Running a honky-tonk, and brazen about it, too. Pure D brazen. Pizazz, my foot. I call that twitching your tail. I said to Essie Mae the other day . . . Essie Mae, I said—"

"Excuse me, Miss Beulah," Paul said, interrupting her endless flow of words. He left Miss Beulah in the parlor, still talking. The screen door was vibrating on its hinges from Martie's flamboyant exit. He flung it open and stepped into the October brightness. A flash of scarlet announced Martie's retreat down the sidewalk. He started to follow and then hesitated. The wonderful thing that had been blossoming between them was squashed the minute Miss Beulah had opened her mouth about a honky-tonk. Now was not the time to force the issue, he decided. And anyway, Miss Beulah was still in his parlor, probably still talking. He sent a prayer winging upward for patience as he turned to walk back into the parsonage.

Martie's blood roared in her ears as she marched down the sidewalk. She heard the screen door slam again and knew Paul was standing in the doorway. If he tried to follow her, she fumed, she'd knock him in the dirt! Her sandals slapped angrily against the sidewalk. Well, why wasn't he following her? It just proved her point: she was totally unsuitable for a minister. She knew it and he knew it. Why then did it make her so angry that he thought so? She was so mad that she could have jumped the cyclone fence flat-footed.

She barreled down the sidewalk, blind to nature's stunning display of gold-dipped foliage.

She rounded the corner of the block and raced up the street to her own house. Baby met her with a short, joyful bark, tail thumping madly.

"It's all your fault," Martie said sharply to her puzzled dog. For an instant Baby's tail forgot to wag, but she recovered quickly and pranced off to worry the cat.

Martie stood in the middle of her yard. She was tempted to put her eye to a crack in the fence to see if Paul was still standing on the steps. It would serve him right, she thought angrily. Honky-tonk, indeed! Self-righteous hypocrite.

Her indignation made her feel noble for all of two seconds, and then she wilted. He had never accused her of anything. He had cast no stones. She had acted on impulse, as she always did. But this time it was different. She had the uneasy feeling that she had thrown away something precious.

Well, damn the luck, anyway. She marched to the pile of tattered flowers and gave them a vicious kick. She would never look at another marigold as long as she lived.

Two

Martie woke up with two furry faces peering down at her. Baby and her archenemy, the gray-blue Siamese cat, were on opposite sides of the bed trying to get their mistress to come down to the kitchen for breakfast. "Shoo, you two hellions." She swatted playfully at her pets. "I jazzed until midnight. Go away and let a girl get her beauty rest." She closed her eyes and rolled over. Baby grabbed the white eyelet comforter and dragged it off the bed. "Doggone it, Baby," Martie grumbled. "I'm going to put you in the cellar."

Baby's tail thumped on the polished wooden floor and her tongue lolled out happily.

Martie stretched her arms above her head and yawned luxuriously. She wasn't wearing a stitch of clothing. Even in the dead of winter, she slept with nothing on. The morning sun gilded her perfect body and made a halo of her tumbled hair. She sprang from the bed humming, stepped into a pink silk teddy, and pulled a gaily embroidered Mexican wedding dress over her head. Tying her hair back with a pink ribbon, she bounded down the stairs to her kitchen.

The large, airy room was awash with October sunshine pouring through a row of ceiling-to-floor windows overlooking her backyard. Martie smiled at a pair of sparrows giving themselves a dust bath in her freshly weeded flower bed. Then she spotted the pile of wilted marigolds, and her smile vanished. She whirled around the kitchen, filling pet dishes, mixing a banana-and-yogurt shake, and trying not to think about a certain too handsome minister who lived across the fence. But she thought about him anyway. She thought about the lock of black hair that needed pushing off his forehead. She thought about his quicksilver eyes that crinkled at the corners when he smiled. Most of all she thought about his voice, that wonderful baritone voice full of trumpets and hallelujahs and little-boy laughter.

The first thing she was going to do this morning, she decided, was get rid of that mountain of marigolds. She should have done it yesterday after that business about the honky-tonk. She guessed that she'd hoped they would disappear overnight all by themselves, just float off on a Pontotoc breeze, never to be seen again.

Leaving her yogurt shake half-finished, she marched to her backyard, intent on destroying the evidence of her ill-fated meeting with Paul Donovan. She thought of burying them and then discarded that idea. If she put them in a hole, Baby would just dig them up again. In the end she decided to rake them into a pile with the leaves and burn them. Somehow burning seemed appropriate, a cauterizing of memories.

"Need any help?"

She spun around at the sound of the well-remembered voice. She'd been so intent on her work that she hadn't heard Paul Donovan approach. Leaning casually on her rake, she tried to act as if her heart weren't doing a rumba inside her chest. "Well, well. If it isn't the Reverend Paul Donovan. What are you doing in my yard so early in the morning? Crusading against honky-tonks?"

His smile didn't waver; he had already made up his mind that today he would clear the air with Martie. "Actually," he replied, "I've come for my socks."

"Are you also accusing me of being a sock thief?" she asked.

"Do your eyes always turn the color of pansies when your dander is up?"

The remark pleased her so much that she almost forgot she was mad. She firmly quashed the urge to laugh and thought how hard it was to be mad at a man whose smile rivaled the sun. "Wouldn't your dander be up if I had come into your yard, unannounced, and demanded that you hand over my socks?"

Paul chuckled. "I see your point," he admitted. "Let's start over, shall we?" He could hardly take his eyes off her. It wasn't just the unusual hair and the brightly colored dress, he decided. It was that remarkable spirit bubbling inside her that drew him like a magnet. "The parsonage dryer is on the blink," he said. "While your pet was gathering my flowers, she apparently decided to retrieve my purple socks, too. They're missing from the clothesline."

"Purple socks! You wear purple socks?" The laughter that had been quivering just beneath the surface exploded. Martie never did anything halfway. Now she threw back her head and roared with uninhibited delight. A man who wore purple socks couldn't be all correct stuffiness and stodgy convention, she thought.

"They break the monotony," Paul explained. "Anyhow, I don't dare not wear them. My formidable Aunt Agnes gave them to me last Christmas."

"I'm afraid you'll just have to face up to Aunt Agnes, Reverend Donovan," replied Martie, her eyes still sparkling with mirth. She was having a hard time remembering that the man in her backyard was off limits, and calling him "Reverend" helped . . . but not much. "I don't have your socks."

"Call me Paul, and it's okay about the socks. They were just a good excuse to come over and talk. There are some misunderstandings that we need straighten out."

"About the honky-tonk?" she asked. Her laughter vanished as she remembered the way he had looked yesterday when Miss Beulah had named her house as the source of sin and disgrace. Well, she certainly didn't run a honky-tonk, but that was not to say that she hadn't been in a few. And enjoyed it, too. One of the best times of her life was her stint as a singer with Booty Matthews's country and western band. They had started in El Paso and rattled all over the Southwest in his souped-up camper, performing in one-horse towns and eating canned pork and beans on tin plates under the stars.

She looked at the Reverend Paul Donovan with his radiant smile and his lofty ideals. She was no fool. Although she had never done anything she was ashamed of, she knew that by his standards she was a tarnished woman. Furthermore, she wasn't about to find out how long she could stand the strictures imposed by a relationship with a man of the cloth. She knew herself too well. She was a free spirit, a maverick; living by the rules would smother her. A small sigh of regret passed her lips. If only he weren't so heart-tuggingly appealing. That lock of hair still needed brushing back from his forehead. It took all the willpower she possessed not to reach over and do it herself.

She hardened her heart. "Did you come on your own, Reverend, or did your church send you?"

He knew she was deliberately erecting a wall between them, and he was more determined than ever to crash through and get to know the woman on the other side. He also knew that she was using his title as a barrier between them, but he decided to let that go—for the moment. "I'm not on a holy crusade, Martie," he said, "but I think you would like me to be. Why?"

Paul's forthrightness shocked and unnerved her. She realized that if she had expected to intimidate this man, she'd been mistaken. Instead, it was the other way around. She wished they had stuck to socks. "I have no idea what you're talking about," she lied. It was probably the only time in her life that she had ever felt the need to hide behind a lie.

"I think you do," he said. "You're putting stumbling blocks in our way."

"There is no 'our way,' Reverend. There's your way and mine."

"And never the twain shall meet?"

"Precisely."

He threw back his head and laughed in what she considered to be a very unpreacherlike manner. The laughter unnerved her even more than his penchant for total honesty. "Why are you laughing?" she asked.

"I'm thinking what fun I'm going to have proving that you're wrong."

"You are the most forward minister I've ever met."

"Lesson number one, Martie." He quickly crossed the small space between them and took the rake from her hand. Letting it drop to the ground, he put one hand on her shoulder and one on her chin. Gently he tipped her face upward, forcing her to look directly into his eyes. "I'm not just a minister," he murmured. "I'm a man. And don't you forget that."

She felt as if she'd been pulled into the center of a volcano. His eyes seared her face, his hand burned her chin, and the nearness of him blazed through her with a ferocity that made her knees weak. Not for one second since she'd met him had she forgotten that he was a man. Unconsciously her tongue flicked over her lips, and she wondered what he would think if he knew that she wanted to seduce him. Right now. This very minute. She wanted to wind herself around him, pull him down to the browning stubble of grass, and make love with him. In broad daylight she wanted to rip his clothes from his body and run her hands over those magnificent muscles and defy the likes of Miss Beulah Grady to peep through a hole in the fence and label it bad.

In the small eternity his hands were touching her, the thoughts reeled drunkenly through her mind, and she knew that she would have yielded to those impulses if he had not been a minister. So much for going by the rules. How long had she been in his company before her maverick nature had her flouting convention and wanting to do the socially unthinkable? All of ten minutes, she decided. No, she would never forget that he was a man. But she also would not forget that he was a minister.

Paul lowered his hands and shoved them deep into his pockets. He balled them into fists and strained against the fabric so hard that it was a wonder he didn't rip holes in his jeans. He hoped that she had no idea how close she had come to being kissed. Don't push too hard and too fast, he warned himself. Give her time to get used to the idea. Curb that impatience that's been growing inside from the moment she fell from the oak tree into the marigold bed. She reminded him of foxfire, and he knew that foxfire glowed only for those who were patient enough to wait for the right moment.

"When I make a pastoral call, I'm usually invited in," he said pointedly, deftly steering them away from treacherous shoals of dangerous conversation and even more dangerous passions.

"For a neighborly cup of tea?" The words tumbled out breathlessly. He was waving a white flag and she gladly accepted the truce.

"With a generous dollop of cream."

"Will milk do? I never keep cream." She led him into her kitchen and cleared the yogurt shake from the table.

"Since this is going to become a neighborly tradition, I'll bring my own the next time." He leaned back in an antique chair and stretched his long legs before him. "Or perhaps we can train your puppy to go through the hole in our fence and fetch the cream from my refrigerator."

She put the water on to boil and joined him at the table. "I think Baby has done enough fetching to last a lifetime," she said. "I'm really sorry about your socks."

"Don't worry. I'm sure Aunt Agnes will give me some more. Purple socks are her stock in trade. Baby is an interesting name for a dog. How did you come to name her that?"

"I always use baby talk with my animals. When I got her, she was so small and cuddly that I addressed her as Baby. The name stuck."

"That was before you moved to Pontotoc?"

"Yes. Baby was my going-away gift from Booty Matthews. We were in Albuquerque at the time."

"He must have been a good friend of yours, this Booty Matthews." Paul almost held his breath, hoping she would not say that Booty Matthews was more than a friend.

"He was and still is. And he's a darned good musician. I traveled with Booty a year, singing in his band." Martie stuck out her chin defiantly. He might as well know every detail of her tarnished past. Maybe then he would stay on his own side of the fence. She watched the struggle on his face as he tried to decide just what her relationship with Booty had been. It almost made her giggle. Booty was pushing sixty, had the voice and build of a grizzly bear and the personality of a pussycat. He had been a father to her that year, and it had been Booty who had noticed the restless stirrings in her and diagnosed them as a longing for roots. "He's partly the reason I came to Pontotoc."

"I hope I can thank him someday."

Martie was saved by the whistling of the teapot. The preacher was incorrigible, she decided. One minute she felt on safe ground with him, and the next she was spiraling into that volcano once more. It was almost as if—"Ouch!" she cried as she sloshed water on her hand.

Paul had crossed the kitchen before she even knew that he'd left his chair. "Let me see that," he murmured as he took her hand and gently rubbed the reddening spot.

The hot breath of the volcano spewed over her, and she tried to remove her hand from Paul's. "I'm okay," she said quickly. "Really. The water wasn't that hot."

He kept a firm grip on her hand as he reached into the refrigerator and got a piece of ice. "Sometimes these things can get nasty. Where's your dish towel?" Numbly, Martie nodded in the direction of the towel holder. He deftly wrapped the ice and applied the cold compress to her hand. She tumbled over the edge of the fiery furnace, felt the molten heat pour through her body and settle in the apex of her thighs. "Now isn't that better?" His thumb traced shivery circles in her palm as he held the compress in place on the top of her hand.

She thought that the kitchen floor might be even better than the grass in her backyard for a seduction. Oh, help! If she didn't get out of this state of mind soon, she would start a scandal her first week in Pontotoc. "Did they teach this bedside manner at seminary, Reverend?"

He kept the compress on her hand, but the erotic circling in her palm stopped. "I learned first aid from my mother. I have six brothers and two sisters. One of us was always burned or bashed or bleeding. I think that's why Theo became a doctor. It was pure self-defense." He still didn't release her hand.

"And why did you become a minister?" It was more than an idle question. Suddenly Martie wanted very much to know why this man had chosen the ministry.

"To serve, Martie," he said simply. "To serve God and my fellowman."

The honest simplicity of his answer took her breath away. She forgot about her burn and his hand on hers. "I don't run a honky-tonk," she whispered.

"I never believed that you did."

"I teach Jazzercise. That was the music Miss Beulah heard. I practice every evening. My ad will be in next week's paper."

Still holding her hand, Paul led her to the table and gently pushed her into a chair. "Now that the air is clear between us, let's have that neighborly cup of tea," he suggested. "You sit there and I'll pour."

Without protesting she acquiesced and watched him move about the kitchen. His movements were surprisingly graceful for such a big man. He brought the teacups to the table, and they talked of inconsequential things, of the weather in Pontotoc, of Saturday night auctions, and of small community doings. And beneath the surface of their conversation swirled seductions and volcanos and heady carousel music.

Suddenly Paul asked her, "Do you like baseball?"

"I love it," she replied enthusiastically. "Once when Dad and I were living in the south of Georgia, I played first base on a neighborhood team. There was nothing to do in that town except play ball and fight mosquitoes. They didn't even have a movie theater. I've been a baseball fan ever since."

"Great." Paul unfolded his long legs and stood up. "I'm taking you to the Indian summer picnic this Saturday."

"How do you know I want to go?"

"You just said that you love baseball. Besides, it will be a good chance for you to meet people. Thanks for the tea." And he was out the door before she could say yes or no.

She twirled around in her kitchen, her hair flying around her in the sunshine. "Well, heck, why not?" she asked the cat, who had just come in to see what was going on. "What can one little picnic hurt?"

The next day Martie alternated between elation and moodiness. Why hadn't she just told him no right away? she grumbled to herself. She really shouldn't allow herself to get close to him: he was too damned sexy. She whizzed around her newly purchased turn-of-the-century home, attacking cobwebs on the ceiling and dust balls under the beds. She had a tug-of-war with Baby over the mop and finally managed to salvage enough of it to clean the kitchen and bathroom floors to a shine.

Pooh-poohing the old adage that Rome wasn't built in a day, Martie waxed her wooden floors and washed her windows, stopping only long enough to stave off starvation with a tuna sandwich. The sun was sinking into the western horizon when she finally took a breather. She sat on her rickety back-porch steps and listened to the cricket songs in her yard. After a few moments Baby nudged her leg to catch her attention and proudly dropped a prize at her feet.

"Well, hello, you old cuddle bum," she cooed, scratching behind Baby's ears. "What do you have now?" The minute she put her hand on the soggy, dirty object, she knew it was Paul Donovan's purple socks. Or at least the remains. Smothering her laughter, she scolded her pet. "What am I going to do with you, you scalawag?"

For an answer, the golden retriever puppy licked her hand and then bounded off to chase a grasshopper.

Still smiling, Martie jumped up from the steps, shoved the socks into her blue jeans pocket, and raced to the oak tree. She climbed rapidly upward until she was a part of the brilliant sunset sky. Inching her way along a fat limb, she traversed the fence and flattened herself out on the branch just above Paul's former marigold bed. A ring of fragrant tobacco smoke drifted around her head as she parted the leaves . . . and looked directly down into a pair of quicksilver-gray eyes.

Paul removed the pipe from his mouth. "The Cheshire cat, I presume?" he asked, smiling.

"No. Just Baby's messenger mistress. I'm returning your socks."

"Remind me to thank Baby."

"Don't be too hasty with the thanks. Just wait until you see the socks." She clutched the limb, already regretting her impulsiveness in climbing up the tree. She was just asking for trouble, she decided. The best thing to do would be to drop the socks down to him and inch back across the limb to her own yard. Cautiously she let go with one hand and tried to reach into her pocket.

"Aren't you coming down?" Paul asked, obviously amused.

"No," Martie replied firmly. "This is not a social call. Just an errand."

"Then perhaps I should come up," he suggested.

"There's room on this limb for only one."

"Pity."

"Besides, what would Miss Beulah say?"

"She would probably be upset . . ."

"That's an understatement!"

". . . because she's missing all the fun."

One of Martie's legs slipped off the limb and dangled in the air. Deftly, Paul reached up and caught her ankle. "Don't worry, Martie," he assured her. "I won't let you fall. You can turn loose the limb."

Falling was the least of her worries. What really bothered her was how she could keep the flames that were licking along her leg from setting fire to the tree. "I'm not worried. You can let go of my leg."

"And be responsible for you breaking a bone? Not a chance." He gave a tug and Martie came tumbling off the limb into his arms.

The electricity of the contact surged between them, and their eyes widened with the knowledge. For a breathless moment they clung to one another, marveling in the rightness of the touch. Martie molded herself to his broad chest and knew that she was courting disaster. The shape of her burned itself forever into Paul's memory, and he wondered if discretion were, after all, the better part of valor. For the first time since becoming a minister he railed silently against the strict code of conduct that kept him from whisking her off to his bedroom.

Reluctantly he lowered her to the ground, knowing that he would be on his knees a long time trying to reconcile himself to the agonizing slowness of developing his relationship by the rules. He shoved his pipe into his mouth, seeking solace in the familiar routine.

Martie was thankful that the waning daylight prevented Paul from seeing how flustered she was. She didn't quite understand it herself. For Pete's sake, she thought, it wasn't as if she had never been with a man. But not even Rafael, the scintillating Spaniard who had taught her to fight bulls by day and introduced her to fireworks of the flesh at night, had made her feel like this. All trembling expectation and joyful music inside. And she and Rafael had been engaged . . . well, practically.

She stuck her hand into her pocket and brought out the abused socks. "I'm afraid these are beyond repair," she said apologetically. "Baby thoroughly chews every gift that she brings to me."

"I noticed that about the marigold you had tucked in your hair the day we met. Why don't we just give these purple socks a decent burial?" he suggested.

"That's your line of work, isn't it?"

Paul took a long draw on his pipe and stood quietly for a moment before answering. "Partially. Marriages, too. Would you like to talk about my work, Martie?"

"Why do you ask?"

"Because my work seems to be a stumbling block to our . . . friendship."

"Nonsense," Martie declared with a toss of her head. "I'm as friendly as a puppy. I even climbed a tree to return your socks."

"So you did. And also to tell me about the marigolds."

She loved the smile in his voice. The fragrant smell of his pipe tobacco blended with the music of crickets in the October evening, and the peacefulness of the small town wrapped around Martie like a benediction. She could almost believe that she and Paul didn't have irreconcilable differences. Almost. "We even shared tea."

"But not ourselves. I want to know why you climb trees instead of going on the sidewalk the long way around. I want to know what makes you love animals and bright clothes and why you retreat when the conversation gets personal."

"I do not retreat."

He chuckled. "No. But you do make a flamboyant exit."

"Flamboyance is my style. Not . . ."

"Not what, Martie?" he asked gently. "Convention? Dullness? Stodginess?"

"Those are your words, not mine. Furthermore, if you're going to preach, I'm going home."

The rich rumble of his laughter filled the evening air. "It's habit, I guess. Sometimes I get carried away." He shoved the socks into her hand. "Here. You hold these while I get the shovel." He disappeared into the growing darkness, whistling.

"I'm not staying for the burial," she called after him. There was no reply. She looked down at the tattered socks. "Well, damn. Pushy preacher." But she was smiling.

Paul returned with the shovel and started digging in the marigold bed. "I love these Indian summer evenings. Especially in Mississippi. Did you know that Pontotoc is an Indian name?"

"I thought this was a burial. Is it going to be a history lesson, too?"

"You don't like history?" he asked, leaning on the shovel and smiling at her.

"Yes," she replied, momentarily blinded by his smile. "I do. As a matter of fact, my mother was a history teacher. The thing I remember most about her is holding her hand as we walked through the enormous stacks in the library." She paused. "But I don't want to talk about history this evening."

"What do you want to talk about?"

"Nothing. I want to be still and listen to nature's music and just *be*."

"Sometimes that's the best communication of all," he said softly.

They worked together silently, with Paul turning the soft earth and Martie bending down to place the socks in the shallow trench. Their silence lent a kind of dignity to the ludicrous occasion. Paul marveled that he was standing in a warm, tag-end-of-summer evening burying socks when he would ordinarily have tossed them into the garbage can. Instinctively he knew that the woman standing beside him was the reason. She made everything an occasion. Just being with her was a celebration.

Finally he stopped shoveling. "All done," he announced.

"That was such a lovely ceremony I think I'm going to cry." The moon sliver suspended in the darkened sky illuminated a telltale moistness in her violet eyes.

Paul looked at the upturned face, and the shovel in his hand slowly drifted to the ground, forgotten. "Martie?" It was half question, half plea as he lowered his head toward hers. Nothing touched except their lips. The first tentative sweetness blended and washed over them like nectar from the gods, and in its wake came a yearning hunger that ripped through them with the force of a tornado.

Martie pulled back as Paul reached out for her. "I think I had better go."

He stood for a moment, collecting his senses and gathering his patience. "I'll walk you home."

"No. I'll take the short cut." She turned and headed for the overhanging limb of the oak tree. Then, realizing that she couldn't reach it, she looked over her shoulder at Paul. "If you'll just give me a boost . . ."

Without speaking he put his hands around her waist and lifted her onto the sturdy limb. He heard the dry leaves rustle around her as she moved back across the fence. And then, out of the darkness, he heard her voice.

"Good night, Paul."

He stood at the fence listening to the sound of her feet running lightly across the yard, and only when he heard her screen door slam did he respond. "Good night, angel."

Three

A pile of discarded garments lay on the floor. "What do you think, Aristocat?" Martie asked the gray-blue Siamese sitting on the windowsill washing his face. "Too funky?" The indigo cotton shirt she wore hung almost to the knees of the baggy knickers, and when she held up her arm, the raglan sleeve fanned out. "Can't play ball in that," she muttered. Ripping the shirt over her head, she tossed it onto the colorful heap of garments. She stepped out of the knickers, kicked them aside, and walked to her closet. "You'd think I was going for an interview with the queen instead of to a picnic," she grumbled, pulling a red flight-style jumpsuit off the hanger. "If I hadn't already said I would go, I can tell you that I would stay home."

Martie zipped the suit almost up to her neck, then leaned over and lowered the zipper a fraction. She brushed her hair until it shone and then wove a scarlet ribbon in the fat braid that she let hang over one shoulder. "But I guess one little picnic can't hurt." She stepped into a pair of red tennis shoes and whirled to face the cat. "This is absolutely, positively the last time that I see Paul Donovan," she told him. The cat switched his tail and jumped off the windowsill. "That kiss last night should never have happened. I don't care how good it felt, it's just not right. Can you imagine me with a minister? I'd smother to death in boredom." Obviously bored himself, the cat padded across the room and out the door. "A big help you are," Martie called after him.

Still mumbling to herself, she gathered the clothes off the floor and hung them back in the closet. She'd half a mind not to go, she thought, but that would be cowardly. And she was not a coward. She might as well get this behind her and then forget about the preacher. She shook the indigo shirt vigorously and shoved it into the closet. Yessir, that's exactly what she would do.

She banged her bedroom door shut and bounded down the stairs singing, "I'm just a gal who can't say no."

"I certainly hope not." The Reverend Paul Donovan looked up at her and smiled. "The door was open. As a matter of fact, the cat let me in."

Martie clutched the railing with one hand and tried to remember that she was already in the process of forgetting this devastating man. "He hates strangers," she said unsteadily.

With a haughty switch of his tail and a baleful glare at his mistress, Aristocat stalked across the spacious hallway and wrapped himself around Paul's legs in a shameful display of adoration.

Martie watched her cat with amazement. "Judas cat," she scolded, laughing.

"Why don't you introduce us," Paul suggested. "Then we won't be strangers."

Martie descended the stairway and peeled her cat from around his legs. "Aristocat, meet the Reverend Paul Donovan."

He solemnly shook the cat's paw. "You can call me Paul."

Aristocat acknowledged the greeting by purring loudly.

"First my dog makes me a thief, and now my cat makes me a liar." Martie set her cat in the hallway and gave him a playful shove. "Scat, you shameless old reprobate."

Martie and Paul loaded her picnic basket into his steady brown Ford, then laughed all the way to the church grounds. The redbrick Faith Church with its white Corinthian columns sat in a grove of trees beside a winding gravel road. Many of the picnickers had already gathered, and festive sounds of laughter and excited chatter filled the air. The sun cast heated rays on the browning patches of grass, and several people had already abandoned their sweaters.

Heads swiveled in their direction when Paul helped Martie from his car. The buzz of conversation ceased for a moment, then started back with renewed vigor as they made their way across the picnic grounds. In her red outfit, Martie stood out like a cardinal at a convention of sparrows.

Paul stopped along the way to make introductions, and a curious crowd of children tagged along behind them. She turned to smile at the children and instantly became their heroine. They gazed with round-eyed adoration at her beautiful face and hung on every musical word that flowed from her lips.

"I think you've made some new friends," Paul observed, nodding with satisfaction from Martie to the children.

"I hope so," she replied happily. "I've always loved children. We understand each other."

He laughed. "I don't doubt that. There are a few trees around here if you and your new friends want to climb."

"Don't think for a minute that I wouldn't if I wanted to."

He held up his hands in mock surrender. "Not even for a second."

A handsome young couple leading a chubby, curly-haired two-year-old between them stopped beside Paul and Martie. Paul introduced them as Bob and Jolene Taylor and their son, Mark.

Bob took Martie's hand between his. "I'm so glad to see the Reverend enjoying the company of a beautiful woman," he said warmly. "It's about time he got out of that study and had some fun."

"Don't let Bob fool you, Martie," Jolene warned, laughing. "His idea of having fun is staying in the field two more hours to plow the back forty."

Bob shrugged his shoulders and grinned. "What can I say? I'm guilty. But I'm not without my social graces. I grill a mean hamburger." He paused. "Hey! Why don't you two come over next Wednesday? After we eat we'll play cards."

"That's a great idea!" Jolene said.

Martie's eyes widened as she looked at Paul. How could she tell these two sincere people that this was just an interlude, that after today the Reverend Paul Donovan would be out of her life? "Paul?"

"Give us a raincheck on that," Paul said smoothly. "Martie's still moving in."

Jolene sensed that there was more to the interchange between her beloved pastor and the delightful woman at his side than met the eye. She took Martie's elbow. "Here," she said. "Let me show you where to put this picnic basket, and then I'll introduce you to my Thursday morning sewing circle." She gave her husband an affectionate pat on the cheek. "Keep Mark occupied, darling, while I show Martie around." Taking command of the situation, she led Martie to a chattering group of young women. "I hope you can do English smocking. We've been dying for somebody to join our group who can teach us how."

"I hardly know which end of the needle to thread."

"That's all right. You can join us anyhow and tell us how you got that perfectly fabulous figure. I might even give up chocolate for a figure like that."

Martie was delighted with Jolene. Just think, she mused, if she hadn't come to the picnic, she would have missed the opportunity of making this new friend. "I'm starting a Jazzercise class next week. Perhaps you'd like to join."

"Can you promise that I'll discover my waistline?" Jolene asked wistfully.

"Only if you lay off the chocolate."

Jolene led her into a lively group of young women, some with young children, some newlyweds, and some still looking. "Let me introduce you to six more fatties who haven't seen their waistlines in fifteen years."

"Speak for yourself, Jolene," a boisterous redhead called Sam piped up. To Martie she said, "You'll have to watch out for Jolene. First she'll get you into the sewing circle and then before you know it she'll have you roped into five different jobs at the church. She's director of the youth department."

Jolene's brown eyes sparkled as she looked at Martie. "Do you sing?"

"Some," Martie replied cautiously.

"I thought so. We've been searching to high heaven for a director of our youth choir. I'm so glad you came today."

Paul appeared behind Martie and casually draped his arm across her shoulder. "I see Jolene's already drafted you."

The heat of his arm on her shoulder combined with the warm rays of the sun made Martie feel flushed. "Oh, dear. I didn't say yes, did I?" Her eyes were wide with appeal as she looked around the circle of women.

"With Jolene, you don't have to say yes," Sam told her. "If you're breathing, she takes it as an affirmative answer."

Paul laughed. "That's right. We're trying not to let Uncle Sam get wind of her. Just think what she could do for the draft, let alone détente." Playfully he flicked Martie's shining braid. "The baseball game is getting ready to start."

"Good." Martie clapped her hands with delight. "I want to play first base."

Sam and Jolene exchanged glances. "Didn't you tell her, Reverend Donovan?" Sam asked.

"Tell me what?" demanded Martie.

"The women are always the spectators," Sam said dryly.

"Why?" Martie put her hands on her hips and looked from Paul to the circle of women.

"Tradition, I suppose," Paul explained. "That's the way it's been since I moved here five years ago."

Martie thrust out her chin and looked defiantly up at Paul. "Hang tradition. I came here to play ball."

"Then why don't you play on my team?" Paul asked her. He admired her spunk. There was no doubt that this turn of events would make a few waves among the more conservative church members, but perhaps that wouldn't be a bad thing. Churches, like people, could become too tradition bound. And when that happened, growth stopped. This spunky, high-spirited woman was not only the best thing that had ever happened to him, she just might be the best thing that ever happened to this church. "Anybody else want to play on my team?" he asked the group.

"I'm going to let Martie pave the way," Jolene said. "Maybe next time."

"Well, shoot," Sam grumbled. "If I had known that I was going to be let in on all the fun, I would have worn something besides this tight skirt and these dad-blamed fussy shoes." She punched Martie affectionately on the arm. "Go get 'em, girl. Hit a home run for me."

"Don't worry. I intend to." Martie tugged Paul's arm. "Come on, Preach. Let's play ball."

Martie didn't hit one home run. She hit three. She was like a match in a warehouse full of fire-works: she ignited the entire assembly of picnick-ers. The chidren went wild with cheering for their colorful new heroine; the liberals, mostly young men and women with a sprinkling of old-timers here and there, felt revitalized; and the die-hard conservatives, led by Miss Beulah and egged on by Miss Essie Mae, searched their vocabularies for new and appropriate ways to pronounce sin and disgrace.

"Did you see the way she slid into home plate?" Miss Beulah sniffed, fanning herself vigorously with a funeral parlor fan. "Just like a *man*. I do vow and declare that I don't know what this younger generation is coming to." She nearly toppled her lawn chair as she turned to look at her companion, Essie Mae Bradford. "Pass me that lemonade, Essie Mae. I think I'm having a prostra-tion attack."

"Lord, Beuler!" Essie Mae always pronounced Miss Beulah's name with an "r." "Hang on. Somebody'll have to issue mouth-to-mouth." Her protrusive eyes began to water at the thought. She had never seen mouth-to-mouth, but she had always fancied that it would be rather erotic. Hastily she poured the lemonade and nearly dropped the glass as she passed it to her friend. "Lord, Beuler! Would you just look at that!" The ball game had ended, and a jubilant Martie had flung her arms around the Reverend Paul Donovan's neck. "If that zipper of hers comes down one more hair, she'll be showing everything she's got." Essie Mae leaned forward in her lawn chair to get a better view. "Shameful! Right in the public view. Lord, Beuler!" She clutched her companion's arm. "I do believe the preacher likes it!"

And indeed he did. The woman with the smudged face and the sparkling eyes who had catapulted herself into his arms for a victory hug reminded him of a delightful, slightly naughty child. He squeezed her briefly and set her on her feet, but that fleeting contact was enough to banish all thoughts of Martie as a child. The high, perfect breasts pressed against his chest set his pulse to racing. Quickly he turned to accept the congratulations of the men on the losing team, but his eyes followed the sprite in the red jumpsuit. Her laughter floated back to him like music as she became the center of an admiring crowd.

As soon as he could, and with what would probably be construed as indecent haste, Paul made his way to Martie. He knew that his life came under close scrutiny because of his position. Sometimes that bothered him, but not usually. His faith kept everything in perspective, and through the years he had developed a remarkable patience that allowed him to weather minor storms of controversy with a minimum of damage, either to himself or to his work.

He linked his arm through Martie's. "I hope you worked up an appetite. This Indian summer picnic is famous all over northeast Mississippi for the food we spread."

"I could ruin that reputation in one fell swoop. How do you think your parishioners will feel about tofu and alfafa sprout sandwiches?" she asked mischievously.

He hesitated. "It sounds . . . intriguing. I can't speak for the rest of the congregation, but being a loyal fried-chicken fan I'll have to be won over."

Martie picked up her basket and looked around the picnic grounds. "Now what?"

"Everybody puts the food on those tables under the oak tree, buffet style. Then you can choose what you want. I highly recommend Jolene's chocolate pie."

As Martie placed her sandwiches on the table, she watched Paul with his parishioners. He stood as solid as a rock in their midst, chatting, counseling, sharing a joke, sharing a burden. His quick laughter and peaceful spirit drew the people toward him, and Martie knew that she was seeing the man at his work. Ministry was not a Sunday morning job; it was seven days a week, twenty-four hours a day. Paul was a heart-thumpingly appealing man; no doubt about it. But he was also a minister, and that was something that could not be left in a briefcase at the office.

Martie heaved a big sigh for what might have been. She had no illusions about the unsuitability of a relationship with a minister. As a free spirit—a maverick of sorts—she knew she was impulsive and unconventional to a fault. And that couldn't be packed into a box and stowed somewhere, either. She unwrapped her sandwiches with unnecessary vigor. Sometimes life just didn't seem fair.

"Those sandwiches look . . . *unusual.*" Miss Beulah's voice interrupted her thoughts. "What are they?"

"Tofu and alfalfa sprouts," Martie told her.

"Alfalfa! Like they feed *cows*?" Miss Beulah swatted the air with her funeral parlor fan, and the red roses on her dress jiggled up and down. "That sweet little Glenda the preacher used to date always brought fried chicken."

Martie's heart plummeted. Paul had said that he was a fried-chicken fan. He was probably a Glenda fan, too, and she had just dreamed all this magic between them, and why did that matter so much because, after all, she was going to forget him after today, and Miss Beulah had just made her as mad as hell. "It's health food, Miss Beulah," she explained sweetly, "but occasionally a cow does eat my sandwiches."

"Well, I *never!*" Miss Beulah made a beeline for Essie Mae to share Martie's latest transgression.

Martie grinned wickedly, even through the blessing, and she was still grinning when Paul led her to a quiet corner under a copse of pines. "This is my favorite spot on the church grounds. Sometimes when I need to think, I leave my office and come here." He spread the blanket he had retrieved from the trunk of his Ford and sat down with his heaping plate.

"It would be a wonderful place to make love," Martie observed, her violet eyes sparkling with devilment.

Paul choked on his bite of fried chicken. What was she up to now? he wondered. He could see the imp peeping through her eyes and decided that silence would be the best response. Let her have enough time to vent whatever was on her mind.

"Once down in Tijuana I did the fandango on top of Rafael's bar. I was dancing so hard my earrings fell into the guacamole dip. Afterward everybody at the party drank champagne from my slippers."

He still didn't say anything.

"Aren't you shocked?" she asked, turning to look at him.

"Am I supposed to be?"

Damn. This was not at all the way she had planned it. He was supposed to see how unsuitable she was and walk off in disgust. It would be easier that way. "Don't you even want to know who Rafael is?"

"Do you want to tell me?" he asked, taking another bite of fried chicken.

"He's a bullfighter. He taught me how to fight bulls and drive fast cars and gamble."

"Do you want me to pass judgment? I'm afraid I'll have to disappoint you."

She thrust her chin out defiantly. "And when I was with Booty, I sang in honky-tonks. Honky-tonks are fun."

"I think so, too," Paul agreed cheerfully.

"You do?"

He smiled. "Yes. I like that kind of music. Lively and earthy, with a toe-tapping beat."

"You go to honky-tonks?" Martie asked, surprised.

"I have. In the restless days of my youth. Did you think I lived in cotton wool before I entered the ministry?"

All her bravado was gone. How could she have believed that this solid, sensible man would turn tail and run? He was not the running kind. If she wanted to end an improbable relationship before it ever started, she would have to do it the adult way. With honesty, not games. But not yet. "What did you do before you entered the ministry?"

"My brother, Tanner, and I were the stars of the Greenville High School football team," Paul replied. "We were also the biggest hellions in the Delta. The world was our oyster, and we were both headed for the big time—pro ball." He put his plate on the edge of the blanket, took his pipe from his pocket, and slowly tamped in the fragrant tobacco. "Life got in the way," he continued slowly. "Dad was killed in an accident, and there wasn't enough money to send two boys to college. Tanner went. I stayed." He smiled down at Martie. "He plays for the Dallas Cowboys and I'm a minister."

"Was ministry second best?"

"No. Life has a way of closing one door and opening an even better one. I'm exactly where I want to be, doing a job that I love."

Martie picked at her sandwich. "You know that I was playing a game with you."

"Yes," he said quietly. "I just don't know why."

"Miss Beulah made me mad. She called my sandwiches cow food." She took a small bite, and her eyes twinkled as she chewed. "Now that she's mentioned it, darned if the alfalfa sprouts don't taste like weeds."

"I thought so, too, but I wouldn't dare say it. Not after seeing the way you can wield a baseball bat." He leaned against the tree trunk and puffed contentedly on his pipe. "You were right about this place," he murmured. His eyes were half-closed, and only the crinkling of laugh lines in his bronzed face gave him away.

Martie nearly bit her finger. She had a sudden vision of the two of them writhing in ecstasy on the carpet of pine needles with nothing except the stars and the whispered breezes to keep them company. She jumped up from the blanket. If she didn't put that city block between them quickly, she wouldn't be held responsible for what she might do.

Paul's hand snaked out and caught her wrist. Pulling her down beside him, he commanded quietly, "Stay."

For a set of legs that had just negotiated three home runs, hers were acting in a mighty treacherous fashion, she decided as she sank down beside him. She was close, too close. The heady fragrance of his pipe tobacco mixed with the clean smell of pine needles made her feel languid and content. She wanted to put her head on his broad shoulder, wrap her arms around his chest, and purr like Aristocat.

Instead she inched away so that her leg was barely touching his blue-jeaned thigh. Even so, his body heat jumped across the small space and melted her all the way down to her toes.

"You forgot to tell me why you've traveled so extensively and why you settled in Pontotoc," he said softly.

"You forgot to ask."

"I'm asking."

At least he wasn't still talking about making love on the pine needles. She supposed that she could endure the pleasant agony of his nearness long enough to carry on a polite conversation without drooling. "Dad's a groundwater hydrologist. After Mom died, when I was seven, I traveled with him on his consulting jobs. One of the places we visited frequently is near here—Tupelo. But it's too big for me. I had seen Pontotoc . . . liked it . . . and when I decided to buy a house, I remembered the peacefulness of this small town." She shrugged. "So, here I am."

Paul shook his head, smiling. "Amazing. The way life keeps opening doors."

He was doing it again—implying that she was a part of his future. Now was the time for that adult honesty she had resolved to use. "Or slamming them shut." She tilted her head to one side, and the shiny braid swung with the motion. "It's been a lovely day, Paul, but you must know that I'm not one of your open doors. We're too different." She waved her hand to encompass the redbrick church, the picnic grounds, and the parishioners gathering their baskets to go home. "I could never be a part of all this, because I don't play by the rules. I would shrivel up and die of frustration if I were forced to."

"I never figured you for a coward."

"I'm not a coward," she snapped. "I'm just facing the simple truth."

Paul reached out and took her hand between his. "Time has a wonderful way of working things out. Why don't you wait and see what happens?"

"I don't have to wait. I know what would happen. I would turn your life upside down and you would try to fit me into a neat little convention-bound cubbyhole." She pulled her hand out of his and jumped up. "And besides, there's Glenda. Why didn't you tell me about sweet little Glenda and the fried chicken? I'll bet she never did the fandango in her life!" All the pent-up frustration came tumbling out. It was not that she was jealous of Glenda, she told herself, it was just that Glenda and her fried chicken were considered *suitable*.

Paul tried to keep a serious face. "No, Glenda never did the fandango. She wouldn't even waltz."

"You see!" Her braid was twitching she was so mad. "Sweet little Glenda probably wouldn't have touched a baseball bat with a ten-foot pole."

Paul unfolded his long legs and stood up. "It's highly unlikely," he agreed solemnly.

Martie folded her hands across her chest and thrust her chin out—her fighting stance. She didn't stop to question her fierce reactions. "Whatever happened to this paragon of suitability? Did she ride off into the sunset on a fried drumstick?"

He could no longer suppress his grin. "No. She rode off to Tijuana with a bullfighter."

His quick wit defused her anger. As her hands dropped to her sides, she shot him an impish grin.

"I don't suppose anybody will ever call me sweet little Martie."

He tilted her chin with his forefinger. "Beautiful.
Seductive. Spicy. But not sweet." His finger traced
the stubborn line of her jaw. "Glenda is a nice girl
that I knew once. She's a part of my past just as
Rafael and Booty are a part of yours. Not my present and not my future." He paused to tuck a stray
curl behind her ear. "There are about fifty people
out there waiting to speak to me before we leave.
Sit tight, angel. I'll be right back."

"I'm no angel, Paul."

He seemed almost not to have heard her as he
took a long draw on his pipe and gazed beyond her
toward the ivy-covered walls of the redbrick
church. "I know. Perhaps that's a part of your
fascination."

She watched him walk across the grass and
become a part of the vine-covered-cottage-and-
picket-fence crowd. He was one with them, chatting and laughing and reminding her of slippers by
the fire and barbecues in the backyard. Bullfights
in Mexico and nightclubs in Texas and skydiving
in California lost their appeal. She looked at his
face and thought of cricket songs and cream in the
tea and moonlight kisses. "Perhaps that's *your* fascination," she whispered. And she knew that the
Reverend Paul Donovan would be very hard to
forget.

Four

Martie mopped the perspiration from her brow and turned up the volume on her stereo as if the increased decibels could wipe Paul from her mind. She stretched and lunged to the frantic beat of the music. "I shouldn't have had that sinfully rich chocolate pie," she said to nobody in particular.

Olivia Newton-John's recorded voice encouraged her to get physical.

"That's what I wanted to do," Martie panted. "But you know how it is with small-town gossip."

She did five rapid waist bends and went into a series of toe touches. "I'm just too physical for him. I mean, can you imagine love in the afternoon with fifty Miss Beulahs pounding on the parsonage door?" Her hands froze on the floor as she peered between her legs at the amused face of Paul Donovan.

"Do you always talk to records?" He was leaning

casually against the door frame, looking very much at home and obviously enjoying the view.

The blood rushed to her head. He looked every bit as good upside down as he did right-side up. "Don't you ever knock?"

"I did, but you didn't hear me. Apparently you were engaged in scintillating conversation." His smile broadened as he moved away from the door and eased his big frame into a straight-backed chair. His mind commanded him to do those things, and it was a good thing that he'd had lots of practice or he would have missed the chair. What was that daring little outfit she was wearing? he wondered. He thought it had something to do with animals, lions or tigers or something, but mostly it had to to do with his heart. It's a wonder they didn't hear its beat clear to Faith Church. And the glistening little bead of sweat that had just rolled between her perfect breasts was the most provocative thing he had ever seen. He stuck one of his shaking hands into his pocket and fetched his pipe. Anything to get his mind off the stunningly sexy woman upended before him. He stuck his pipe into his mouth, then forgot to light it.

Martie slowly straightened up. "I suppose the cat let you in." She walked across the large, almost bare room and got a towel from the chest beside the exercise barre.

Paul watched her move and took a long, steadying draw on his pipe. He still didn't know it was unlit. "No," he mumbled. As conversation went it wasn't much, but it was the best he could do under the circumstances.

She wiped her damp forehead with the towel and tried to pretend that his voice wasn't sending shivers up and down her spine. "Then who let you in?" she asked.

He took another draw on his pipe and suddenly

realized it wasn't lit. Removing the pipe, he performed that small chore with a sense of amazement at the strange malady that had stricken him since Martie had come to town. "Actually, I was standing on your porch steps looking forlorn and Baby came to my rescue. She pushed the door open and then turned around to invite me in."

"Are you an interpreter of barking?"

"No. I'm a tail-wagging interpreter." The words bounced innocently around the silent room, and the Reverend Paul Donovan nearly bit the stem of his pipe in two.

Martie covered her laughter by burying her face in the towel. The grandfather clock in the hallway chimed seven, and somewhere in the ancient house Aristocat, who rarely spoke unless he had just cause, gave Baby a sound scolding. Olivia Newton-John still exhorted everyone to get physical, and Martie wanted to but knew that she didn't dare because Paul was a minister. She hung the towel on the rack and unconsciously tilted her chin up. As they say in the movies, she told herself, it was time for plan B, whatever that was. She didn't have a plan B, but Paul didn't know that, and she could be very inventive when she tried.

"I hope you're not too big on Southern hospitality," she told him.

"I haven't given it much thought lately."

"You probably will after this evening," she continued firmly, "because I'm showing you the door."

"I've already seen it." His smile was perfectly innocent, but his eyes twinkled with devilment.

She was too busy trying to invent plan B to notice. She paced as she talked, emphasizing her words with gestures and tosses of her head. "I'm not going to see you anymore because I'm forgetting you."

He wanted to take her in his arms and kiss the

silver-blond curl that rested at the nape of her neck. Instead he said, "Why?"

"Because of the picnic this afternoon," she promptly replied.

"I thought you enjoyed the picnic."

"Well, actually, it was because of the tofu and the fried chicken and the polyester pants suits."

"You lost me after the tofu."

"Don't you see!" Arms akimbo, she stopped in the middle of the floor and glared at him. "I'm different."

Paul thought she looked about as formidable as a china doll. "You certainly are. What do you call that outfit you're wearing?"

"It's a leotard and you're as stubborn as a post oak."

"Tenacious, too," he agreed cheerfully. "I already told you that."

Plan B wasn't working. She studied the toe of her hot-pink ballerina slippers. Impossibly long lashes concealed her eyes, and she didn't know that her vulnerable pose ripped at Paul's heart and threatened to topple his shaky reserve.

When she lifted her head, her violet eyes looked as if they'd been drenched in sunlight. "Why are you here?" she asked softly.

"I was sitting in my study going over tomorrow's sermon when I felt a compelling urge to see you." He rose from his chair, tamped out his pipe, and moved toward her with slow, deliberate movements. "Your thoughts came winging to me across the fence, and I knew, as if you were in the same room, that you were busy erecting walls." He stopped only inches from her, and his magnificent voice swept over her in quiet seduction. "I won't let you get rid of me that easily." His hands reached out and captured her shoulders. "I won't let you forget me, Martie."

She lifted her face to his and suddenly they were in each other's arms, pressing and tasting and probing and swaying with the whirlwind that overtook them. Her fingers curled into his hair and she arched upward to meet the demanding thrust of his tongue. Paul made a sound that was half agony, half ecstasy as he hauled her against his body, fitting her to his hard planes and muscular ridges. Walls crumbled and reserve flew out the window as they clung together, savoring the magic that bound them.

Time stood still for them—but not for the rest of the world: crickets sang in the October evening; Baby sneaked through the fence to see what she could find on the preacher's clothesline; Aristocat sat on the fence serenading Miss Beulah's prissy Persian; Jolene and Bob put catsup on their grilled hamburgers; Sam sprayed bug guard in her yard; and Essie Mae trained her binoculars through a gap in her hedge to see what the Bishops were up to. And inside Martie's house the hall clock chimed the half hour.

Pontotoc and its residents could have dropped off the map and the two people in the exercise room would never have noticed. They were in another world, a world filled with splendid heat and yearning flesh and unbearable longing. Theirs was an urge as ancient as time, and it was all the more poignant because it was forbidden.

Paul was the first to break away. Shaking his head slowly to clear his drugged senses, he let his arms drop away from Martie's irresistible form. He took a step backward, putting a breathing space between them.

Martie ran a trembling hand through her hair and wondered how plan B could have gone so wrong. "You like to play with fire, don't you, Paul?"

"Only since I met you."

"If that was a sample of not letting me forget, you've succeeded. I won't need a second demonstration."

They stood a few inches apart, their breathing combining in harsh cadence in the evening-quiet room, as they pondered their separate dilemmas. The patient minister won a mighty struggle over the restless man, and the impetuous gamine triumphed over the passionate woman.

Martie was the first to speak. The sparkling smile she cast at him transformed her from beautiful seductress to fun-loving little girl. "You want fire?" she said. "I'll give you fire. After tonight you'll be begging me to forget you." She grabbed his hand and dragged him through the rambling house to the kitchen. "Make us two cups of hot chocolate while I change. The cocoa is in the cabinet beside the sink."

Paul laughed indulgently. Again he was reminded of the elusive foxfire as she made a lightning transition from desirable to playful. "How do you know that I like hot chocolate?"

"You look like a hot-chocolate man to me." She bounced out of the kitchen. "Make mine with lots of sugar," she called over her shoulder.

"I know." Alternately whistling and smiling as he worked, he thought about the wonderful providence that had set the woman of his dreams right behind the parsonage fence.

Martie made a detour by the exercise room to shut off the stereo, then bounded up the stairs two at a time to change. Telling herself that this was plan C, or get-rid-of-the-minister-once-and-for-all tactics, she took undue care in selecting a hot-pink camp shirt and aqua cropped pants. She tied a hand-woven sash in rainbow colors around her tiny waist and decorated herself with dangling turquoise earrings, a squash-blossom necklace and

seven silver bangle bracelets, souvenirs of her singing stint with Booty. A little hum bubbled up the
whole time she was dressing.

When she rejoined Paul in the kitchen, she said
in a voice as gay as her attire, "Darned if I didn't
nearly land on my bottom. Is my hot chocolate
ready?"

Paul handed her a cup of the steaming liquid. "I
beg your pardon?"

"I slid down the banister," she explained airily.
"I've always wanted to do that."

He threw back his head and roared with laughter. Had he thought being with her was a celebration? Being with her was a full-fledged party,
complete with balloons and bazookas and confetti.
"Did you get splinters? I'm an expert splinter
picker."

"Perhaps we should check it out, Reverend
Donovan," she said with mock seriousness.

"Don't tempt me."

"You started this conversation, remember?"

"So I did." They sipped their hot chocolate in
companionable silence for a while, and then Paul
spoke again. "I'm consumed with curiosity. Just
what are your plans for making me flee in terror
from my beautiful backyard neighbor?"

"You'll have to wait and see," Martie replied mys-
teriously. "Don't you like surprises?"

"Coming from you, yes. I like everything about
you, Martie."

And she liked everything about him, she
decided. If only things were different. She plopped
her empty cup on the table and stood up. She was
not one to mourn what might have been. Circumstances couldn't be changed, but feelings could.
Blithely she embarked on the course of alteration.
"Shake a leg, Preacher, or you'll miss all the fun."

The screen door banged shut behind them as

Martie led Paul to her car. It was an aging Thunderbird convertible painted fire-engine red and boasting a four-barrel carburetor that made everything else on the road look like a snail.

Martie slid behind the wheel. "Hang on to your hat, Paul." The revving of the engine resembled the roar of fifteen lions.

"I'm not wearing one."

"Then hang on to your head," she warned him as she barreled out of her driveway and careened madly down Highway 6 toward Tupelo. Two vans and a Pepsi-Cola truck blurred together as she whipped around them and zoomed down the road.

"Do you always drive like this?" Paul asked mildly.

"No," she yelled over the wind that whistled around their heads. "Sometimes it's better."

"Better?"

"Faster."

He shook his head and prayed.

They came to the Wal-Mart on the western side of Tupelo and clipped down the Main Street at a sprightly pace. Heads turned to look at the bright woman in the bright car, and Martie waved at everybody, whether she knew them or not. At crosstown she turned right and zipped down Gloster. Late Saturday night shoppers and moviegoers turned to watch their progress, and many speculated that a celebrity had come to town, for surely no one else would dare drive that way.

The tires of the red Thunderbird squealed as Martie swerved right onto Garfield and wheeled into Matoka Park. She bounced out of the car, put her hands on her hips, and looked up at Paul. "If you think that was something," she said, "just wait 'til you see the way I drive a go-cart."

"As long as I'm not the passenger." His legs were wobbly and he was still praying.

"Passenger, shoot! You're the other driver." She grabbed his hand and tugged him up the hill.

"I haven't been in one of those things since I was twelve," he protested.

"You don't know what you've been missing!"

"You ride go-carts regularly?" He didn't know why that should surprise him.

"I ran the Happy Day Care Center in Beaumont, Texas, for a while," she explained. "I frequently took the children to amusement parks. Of course, they were just an excuse so that I could ride go-carts and water slides. I adore amusement parks. I think they keep a person young at heart."

"Would you mind if this young-hearted but definitely old-bodied man sat on the sidelines and watched?" he asked, smiling.

She looked solemnly up at him and repeated the words he had said to her at the picnic. "I never figured you for a coward."

He paused. "All right . . . I accept the challenge. Lead on, angel." He affected the long-suffering look of a horse thief being led to a hanging.

"I intend to beat your socks off," Martie warned him.

"I've no doubt about that." Paul looked at the kiddie-sized go-cart. "I don't think I'll fit."

"You have to fit. It's no fun if you just watch." She shot him a mischievous look. "Besides, how will I make you want to forget me if you don't suffer? Fold your legs." She smiled as he lowered himself into the tiny car. "A little more." She burst out laughing as he finally managed to squeeze most of himself into the miniature vehicle.

"What's so funny?" Paul asked.

"You should see yourself." She laughed some more. "You look like a pretzel with your knees up under your chin."

"I've had more fun at the doctor's office," he grumbled good-naturedly.

Martie smiled gleefully as she climbed into her car. Her plan was working, she thought. After tonight, the Reverend Paul Donovan would cross the street to get away from her. She looked at his broad back, and her feeling of satisfaction vanished. Without warning a tiny ache started in her chest at the thought of not seeing him anymore and grew until it filled her heart with pain. She looked up at the stars and whispered a remembered childhood phrase. "I wish I may, I wish I might, have the wish I wish tonight." But she knew that it couldn't be so.

She pressed hard on her accelerator and whizzed past Paul's car. Time to get on with the plan. She could think about her loss tomorrow.

Her naturally high spirits reasserted themselves as she drove with daredevil exuberance. Her light hair, washed silver by the moon, whipped out behind her as she tore around the track at breakneck speed, whooping with uninhibited joy. She grinned wickedly as she imagined how appalled the minister would be.

Paul was enchanted.

After the wild go-cart ride Martie challenged him to a game of putt-putt golf. By now she was having so much fun that she had forgotten her original purpose in coming to the park. She smiled and sparkled and spoke eloquently with the body language that he had loved from the first day he'd met her. She was a terrible golf player, so each small triumph was occasion for hand clapping and spontaneous bear hugs.

Paul was bewitched.

"Oh, dear!" she cried. "Just look at that!" Her brilliant smile never wavered as she putted onto the wrong green and turned the mistake into an adventure by making the acquaintance of a seventy-year-old dancing couple from Verona. "You jitterbug! I've always wanted to know how to do that," she told him. And they treated her to an impromptu lesson beside the windmill on the third hole. It took her fifteen minutes to get back to her green.

Paul was delighted.

Being with her, he decided, was like being in sunlight. He felt warm and contented inside, and he knew that he was falling in love. She was a dream, all lush, desirable woman one minute and joyful little girl the next.

Martie resumed her game and promptly knocked her ball over the fence. He stood quietly, puffing on his pipe as he watched her climb after it. Did she have any idea, he wondered, of her remarkable talent for making people love her? She returned triumphantly holding the ball aloft and sporting a hole in the knee of her pants.

"I finally got the little devil," she announced gaily, then picked up her club and prepared to swing. Stopping in midswing, she looked up at him. "What's my score now?"

"Sixty-five over par," he told her.

She pushed her hair back from her face and smeared a streak of dirt on her cheek. "I guess that means I'm losing?"

He resisted the urge to bend down and kiss the smudged cheek. "By a landslide."

"Then I shall treat you to ice cream," she announced grandly. Her club sailed into the air as she gave the ball a mighty whack. "I think I'm going to turn my talents elsewhere."

"Allow me." Paul began to take off his shoes.

"What in the world are you doing?" she asked.

"Have you never heard of gallantry? You insisted

on climbing the fence for your ball. The least I can do is wade a pond for your club."

"Yes, but I like climbing fences. Wading, too."

He put his foot into the cold water and grimaced. "I guess it grows on you."

They finished the game in style, Paul with the bottoms of his jeans legs wet and Martie with a hole in her pants. Her luck changed at the end, and she hit a hole in one.

"I think I finally have the hang of this game," she declared happily.

Paul took her elbow and escorted her back to the car. "I think if you live long enough, you'll be a fairly decent player." He grinned down at her and resisted the urge to ravish her lips.

She slid behind the wheel. "How long is that?" She looked across the car and wanted to devour him piece by piece, starting with that wonderful cleft in his chin. Instead, she revved the engine to life. The wind whipped her already tousled hair as she pulled onto Gloster and silently denounced fishbowl professions and public decorum.

She pulled up at the grand Hilton Hotel and informed him that they were going to have Häagen-Dazs ice cream by candlelight. She expected him to be mortified at the thought of a ragamuffin going to the Ritz, but instead he was delighted with the woman who approached life with such zest.

"Candlelight becomes you," Paul told her as they sat in a snug corner away from the late-night diners.

"You're supposed to be concentrating on your rum raisin," Martie informed him. She took a big bite and rolled her eyes to show him how to concentrate on the ice cream. But tingles were rippling along her spine, and she was having a hard time remembering that certain things were taboo in ritzy restaurants. Things like ripping the shirt off the man beside you and purring against his chest. Or kicking off your shoes and running your bare foot up his pant leg. Or leaning across the table and licking that little dollop of ice cream off his lips.

"I'd rather concentrate on you," he murmured.

"Which part of me?" she asked. "My daredevil driving or my disregard for convention?"

"Neither." His voice wrapped her in velvet. "Your enchanting smile and your incredible eyes." He put down his ice-cream spoon and reached across the table to take her hand. "I'm just sorry about one thing."

"That I'm totally unsuitable. Right?" Part of her wanted him to say yes, but most of her wanted a denial. Her lips were slightly parted as she waited for his answer.

His fingers moved in slow circles on her hand as he sat quietly in his chair savoring her. The candlelight reflecting on her hair gave her an ethereal quality. He smiled, thinking of the many facets of her personality. She was angel and flesh-and-blood mischief-maker, tranquillity and high-voltage energy. She was flamboyant woman with flashy jewelry and gamine with dirt on her cheek. She was endlessly fascinating, and even if he lived to be a hundred, he knew that she would still be surprising him. He thought of the word he and his brothers had used to tease one another about girls when they were growing up—smitten. There was no doubt about it: Paul Donovan was smitten.

"No," he told her in his marvelous deep voice. "I'm sorry you didn't think of this sooner."

"You're not serious! I know you don't spend your Saturday nights this way, racing through the streets like a bat out of hell and wading in ponds and riding in miniature cars."

"The go-carts and the hair-raising ride from Pontotoc notwithstanding, I'm having a wonderful evening. The company makes it so."

"I didn't plan for this to happen," she admitted. "You were supposed to hate this evening."

"You made a common mistake, Martie, thinking that I'm a stick-in-the-mud simply because of my profession."

"I did *not* think that."

Still holding her hand, he smiled. "Not even a little?"

She made a face at him. "Maybe just a teensy bit. Did you learn mind reading at seminary, too?"

"I learned about people long before that. Living with my brothers and sisters, not to mention a host of aunts, uncles, and cousins made home-grown psychology a necessary survival skill. Appearances are sometimes deceiving, and people rarely fit into the neat cubbyholes we assign them."

Martie withdrew her hand from his. "This evening is an exception. A fluke. It doesn't change a thing." She turned her head toward the window so that he wouldn't see her face. He was too discerning, she thought. He would see the uncertainty in her eyes. If the evening had failed miserably as an incentive for forgetting, it had succeeded royally as a vehicle for advancing their romance. Through the window she saw the edge of an orange moon, brilliant as only an October moon could be; and she wondered if the improbability of their relationship was the cause of her fatal attraction. Was she like a child who wanted most what it could not have? She glanced at Paul from under her lashes. No. His inaccessibility was not the attraction. It went deeper than that. He was quiet strength and controlled energy, easy companionship and heart-thundering sensuality. And she wanted to climb across the table and ravish his made-for-kissing lips.

"I agree." Paul's voice pulled her out of her reverie. "It doesn't change a thing. I'm a minister and you're a Jazzercise teacher, and we still live across the fence from each other." Something changed in his eyes, as if a wonderful secret were lurking in their depths. "And something has already been set in motion between us. Something neither of us can stop."

She thrust her chin out stubbornly. "I intend to try."

"Did you two enjoy the ice cream?" Neither of them had heard the waitress approach.

"Yes, thank you," Paul told her.

She stuck a pencil into her red topknot and gathered the empty bowls onto a tray. "I told Mary Muldooney back there in the kitchen that I never saw a couple have more fun over two little dishes of ice cream. Been married long?"

Martie opened her mouth to speak, but the waitress didn't require an answer. She had long ago learned the art of carrying on one-way conversations. "Mary Muldooney says you are probably honeymooners, but I told her you looked more like one of them fairy-tale couples where everything is just so combustible. You know what I mean?" They didn't have the foggiest idea, but that didn't stop Ethel Ann. She rarely had a captive audience, which translated meant one too polite to get up and leave; and when she did, she took full advantage. Shifting the tray to her hip, she leaned down to wipe the table. "Now you take the Westgates," she continued. "Fight like cats and dogs. Even in public. Now I ask you, is that any way to live?" She didn't wait for their answer, of course. "It's as plain as Yankee Doodle that you two palpitate for one another. And besides that have the highest admo-

nition for each other. You know what I mean?"
They still didn't. Ethel Ann reached into her pocket
for the check and waved it in the air as she continued her monologue. "This world would be a better
place if more married folks remembered that. Palpitation and admonition. And it all starts and ends
in the bedroom." She winked at Paul. "Right,
honey?"

Paul was equal to the occasion. "I couldn't agree
with you more. . . . You didn't tell us your name."

"Ethel Ann, honey." She trained her bright
copper-penny eyes on Martie. "Starts and ends in
the bedroom," she repeated drolly, and then she
headed toward the kitchen to gossip with Mary
Muldooney.

Paul and Martie hurried from the restaurant.
"Do you think we're combustible?" Martie asked,
shooting Paul a pixie smile.

"Not to mention palpitating," he said, with a
straight face. They laughed all the way to the parking lot.

Suddenly Martie grabbed his arm. "Paul, I
almost forgot."

"What?" he asked, covering her hand with his.

"We can't leave the Hilton without riding the
glass elevator."

"I should think not," he solemnly agreed.

So they made their way to the electronic glass
cage that whisked them toward the stars. Paul
pulled her into the circle of his arms, and she
leaned there as naturally as if it were an old habit.

"You see that constellation?" She pointed to the
Big Dipper. "After Mom died I imagined that she
was up there, riding in the dipper, and that if I
concentrated hard enough, she would know what I
was thinking. Even after I learned better, I still felt
that the stars somehow brought me closer to her."

Paul tightened his arms around her in silent

understanding. And even after the elevator had returned them to firm ground, their thoughts were still up among the stars.

Martie yawned hugely as they stood beside her red car. "Too much activity for one day," she apologized.

"I'll drive home." Both of them thought how right "home" sounded. How natural. As if they were an old married couple on the way to a session of Ethel Ann's palpitation.

Once home, Paul deposited Martie on her back-porch steps, then gathered her into his arms and kissed her until they were both breathless.

"Good night, Martie," he murmured. Then, without another word, he walked away.

She watched until he was a faint shadow in the night. "Good-bye, Paul."

Church chimes echoed in the morning air as Martie sprinted down the sidewalk in her neon-bright jogging suit, Baby hard at her heels. "Morning, Miss Beulah," she called, setting her rainbow-hued bangle bracelets ajingle as she waved.

Miss Beulah looked up from the water dish she was filling for her Persian, Falina Theona. In her brown velour housecoat she looked like a fat partridge as her head swiveled on its squat neck to watch the progress of Pontotoc's Jezebel. "Brazen creature," she sniffed. "And on a Sunday morning, too."

Martie whizzed down the sidewalk, turned a corner, realized she would pass the parsonage, and turned in the other direction. She didn't need any more reminders this morning, she mused. Today she was definitely, positively, without a doubt forgetting the minister. She pushed herself, jogging five miles instead of her usual four. Ordinarily she would have selected a church, for she loved Sunday morning services. But not today. Not yet. Being in church, even if it were not his, would have reminded her of Paul.

She was wheezing when she completed her morning workout and plopped down on her back-porch steps. "I don't know what's wrong with me," she wondered aloud. "I guess I didn't sleep too well last night." She rubbed Aristocat's shiny coat.

He endured the attention briefly before walking away to sit in his favorite spot by the birdbath. Baby, who thrived on affection, bounded around the corner of the house, bringing yet another gift to his mistress.

Martie absently scratched her puppy's head as she contemplated the fence that separated her from the parsonage.

"If I didn't already love this house and this town, I would move," she confided to her pet. "It wouldn't be the first time." Her hand moved to stroke the healthy pelt on Baby's back. "But even if I went to the moon, I would still remember the way he smiles with his eyes . . . and the sound of his voice . . . and the way he looks in the moonlight."

The loose skin sagged around Baby's face, giving her a mournful look as she lifted her head to study her mistress. Suddenly she gave a sharp bark.

Martie looked from her pet to the soggy offering at her feet. Gingerly she lifted the mangled garment. "Good grief!" she cried. "The minister's shorts!"

Five

Paul, in clerical collar and black robe, sat behind the pulpit and scanned the church pews for Martie. As the organ swelled to a mighty crescendo, his heart plummeted. There was no silver-blond head among the congregation. The joining of the congregation and the organ in a majestic "Amen" brought his thoughts back to the service. He lifted his eyes and whispered, "I'm only human, Lord."

Martie spent most of the day moving the preacher's shorts around. First she tossed them into the garbage can. Then, feeling cowardly, she fished them out and left them in a soggy heap beside the back door. Something would definitely have to be done about them, she decided; she just couldn't figure out what that something was.

She selected her favorite book of Walt Whitman

poetry and carried it to the sunroom. But right in the middle of "Sometimes with One I Love" she put the book down, marched through the house, and picked up Paul's shorts. They were still damp from Baby's mistreatment. She looked inside the waistband at the label: Medium, 32–34. Just what she'd thought. The shorts dangled from her hand as she considered the possibilities of Medium, 32–34, all of them attractive.

Then, feeling guilty, as if she had barged unannounced into his bedroom and seen him naked, she put the shorts into her washing machine and started the cycle. As she dumped in the detergent she decided to return the clean shorts via the tree.

While the shorts washed she had an afternoon snack and revised her plan. She would put them in a box and send them to him by mail. An act of cowardice, but necessary for self-preservation.

She changed the shorts to the dryer, then returned to the sunroom, where she picked up her book and tried to immerse herself in Walt Whitman. The shorts kept intruding. Even her favorite, "Out of the Cradle Endlessly Rocking," couldn't completely occupy her mind. By the time she got to the line, "A thousand warbling echoes have started to life within me, never to die," she knew what those echoes were. They were Paul's shorts, screaming evidence of the man she was trying to forget.

She replaced the book on the shelf and transferred the shorts from the dryer to a shelf in the closet. But even with the door shut, they still warbled at her. She snatched them out again and decided to patch the holes Baby had made. Sewing was not her forte, but she had never seen anything that she couldn't try at least once. She had a moment of indecision over whether to use the red or the green thread, those two being the only colors available; but once she had selected the red, she tackled the project with enthusiasm.

The shorts were well worn and getting a little threadbare on the seat. They felt soft and pliable in her hands. From time to time she glanced up from her sewing and smiled. It was a dreamy smile, incorporating visions of Medium, 32–34, and palpitations that began and ended in the bedroom.

She pricked her finger twice and got the thread so tangled once that she had to pull it all out and start over. When the project was finally finished she held it up for inspection. Nothing could get through the holes, that was for sure. She actually blushed at the image that thought aroused. But pulling the torn places together had altered the dimensions of the shorts so that one side was decidedly smaller than the other. Martie tilted her head and studied her handiwork. She thought the red thread and the new proportions gave the shorts a rakish quality. Leaving them in her wicker rocker, she went outside for a breather.

The sun was beginning to drop low in the western sky, and there was a nip in the air. Indian summer would soon be over, she thought. She wrapped her arms around herself for warmth and strolled past her birdbath toward the large floribunda rosebush that was still blooming profusely. As she began to gather a bouquet, a spiral of fragrant tobacco smoke wafted over the fence. She straightened up and looked in that direction. Paul must be on the other side of the fence smoking his pipe, she decided. She would recognize that smell anywhere.

With a thousand warbling echoes still stirring within her in spite of her efforts to silence them, she moved toward the fence, and the forgotten roses drifted to the ground in her wake. A good-sized peephole presented itself, and Martie bent down and put her face to the opening.

Paul was standing with his hands in his pockets, puffing on his pipe and looking at the sunset. He was the picture of contentment and tranquillity.

An intense longing that had been shimmering inside her all day welled up and burst forth. "Paul!" she called.

He turned toward the fence and removed his pipe. "I seem to be hearing angel voices."

"It's just me."

In the waning light he could see one eye and the tip of her nose through the hole in the fence. "I'm relieved," he said, and smiled. "Disembodied voices don't usually come with freckled noses." He walked so close to the fence that the wide expanse of his shirtfront filled Martie's view.

"My nose is not freckled," she protested, laughing. Paul always made her forget her original intentions.

"I see one. Right there." He touched her nose with the tip of his finger.

"Oh, that. It's kind of pale, isn't it?" she asked hopefully.

"Yes."

"Good. I've always disliked those freckles, so I pretend they don't exist."

There was a silence on the other side of the fence, and then Paul spoke. "Just as you've been pretending all day that I don't exist?"

"Yes," she admitted. "And it would have worked except for the shorts."

He bent down and put his eye to the crack. "I'm afraid you've lost me."

Startled, she pulled back. "Baby stole a pair of your shorts from the clothesline."

"Which ones?"

"The blue ones. And Paul . . . they're getting kind of threadbare. Why don't you buy some new ones?"

"I'm just getting those broken in. They're comfortable that way."

Martie reflected that this conversation wasn't nearly as difficult as she had expected. As a matter of fact, she was having fun. Temporarily, of course. "I'm going to mail them back to you. I have to warn you, though; Baby did some damage. But I fixed it with red thread."

She was so serious that he held back his laughter. "I'll come over there and get them."

"No!" she cried.

"Why not?" He was getting a crick in his neck, so he straightened up. The minute his eye vacated the hole, hers was back.

"Because I'm still forgetting you," she replied determinedly. "You can't come over here, and I'm not even going to talk to you anymore."

"Does that mean just in person, or does that include treetop and fence-hole conversations as well?"

"All of them, I think."

"But how will you tell me about Baby's raids on my clothesline?" he asked.

"You can patch the holes in the fence so she can't come over."

"I like it this way. I think I'll let the holes stay."

"Then I'll patch the holes. Good-bye, Paul. And that's my final word."

He chuckled, then called across the fence, "I'm going to pray that you forget to buy the nails, angel."

"I'm not an angel!" she yelled. "And that's really my final word."

Paul stood smiling beside the fence for a long time after he had heard her screen door slam. He could wait, he thought. He knew as surely as the sun rose in the east that Martie was part of his future. The grand design had already been drawn, and neither of them could change it. He might hurry it along, however. He tamped out his pipe, stuck it in his sweater pocket, and headed for the parsonage whistling.

Monday morning Martie went outside to pick up her forgotten roses.

"Good morning, Martie." Paul's rich voice startled her, coming as it did out of nowhere.

She ran to the fence and put her face to the crack. Finding herself nose to nose with the minister, she pulled back. "What are you doing?" she asked.

"Greeting you."

"I'm not talking to you, remember?"

"That's all right. I'm still talking to you. Besides, we didn't finish that conversation about my shorts."

"Reverend *Donovan!*" Miss Beulah Grady had entered his yard unnoticed. Her eyes were glazed with shock at the minister's strange behavior and outrageous remark. "What on earth are you doing?"

Paul straightened up. "Hello, Miss Beulah. I'm having a neighborly chat with Martie."

"Morning, Miss Beulah," Martie called through the fence, grinning impishly. Most of Miss Beulah was not visible through the peephole, but the part that was was heaving with indignation.

Miss Beulah squinted her eyes and tried to see what that brazen woman was wearing, but the hole in the fence was too small and the minister was blocking most of the view. All she saw was a flash of scarlet. She'd give her eyeteeth to know what had been going on when she appeared. Shifting her covered basket from one arm to the other, she spoke with saccharine sweetness. "I've brought the preacher some scones, fresh from the oven. Why don't you come over and join us?"

"That's a wonderful idea," Paul agreed enthusiastically. "Just scoot up the tree, Martie, and I'll help you down on this side."

Miss Beulah's eyebrows shot up into the air at that scandalous suggestion, and all attempts at subtlety vanished. "Reverend *Donovan*! I should think that conduct is highly unseemly for a minister. What if somebody sees? Word would get all over town before the day was out."

A small muscle twitched in Paul's jaw, the only sign of his inward struggle. "I think you've underestimated the good people of this town, Miss Beulah."

Martie was furious and immediately charged full tilt into battle. "I don't believe the Reverend Donovan's reputation needs any defense, Miss Beulah," she declared loudly, "but I'm going to put your mind and your tongue at ease. I have no designs, either scandalous or otherwise, on the minister. The only thing we have in common is a fence. And now, if you two will excuse me, I'm going to clean my honky-tonk." She whirled away from the peephole without waiting to see Paul's face. Covering her ears with her hands, she ran into her house. Don't look back, she told herself. She had burned her bridges, and everybody was better off.

She didn't stop running until she was upstairs. Furiously she ransacked her closet, looking for a box. The only thing she could find was a heart-shaped one that had once held candy. Grabbing the mended shorts from the wicker rocker, she stuffed them into the box and slammed the lid shut. "I'm not going to cry," she said to the small wren sitting on her windowsill. Two fat tears rolled down her cheeks, under her chin, and into the neck of her scarlet sweater. She sniffed as two more followed. "I never cry," she informed the wrens.

On Tuesday Paul went to Baptist Hospital in Memphis to be with a parishioner who was having open-heart surgery, and Martie organized her first Jazzercise class. If thoughts had been birds, a whole flock of them would have been winging their way between Pontotoc and Memphis. While Martie was talking to Jolene about the class, she had a sudden vision of Paul shaking hands with Aristo-cat, and she burst out laughing. And once when Paul went to the coffee machine, he put his money in and stood for five minutes thinking about Martie's hair in the moonlight before he remembered to punch the button.

It was after midnight when Paul returned to Pontotoc, but even then he could hear music coming from Martie's house. It wrapped itself around his heart and squeezed as he was getting ready for bed. He stood at the window for a long time, smoking his pipe and watching the moon create changing patterns of shadow and light on the backyard fence. After the music stopped he went into his study to record a tape. At three o'clock, satisfied with his labors, he finally went to bed.

The heart-shaped box lay open on Paul's kitchen table. He alternately sipped coffee and picked up the mended shorts for another look. But mostly he smiled. Martie's sewing was about on par with her golfing, he thought, but it didn't matter a whit. The bright red thread, jumbled into knots and crisscrossing the faded blue shorts, was just like the woman who jitterbugged in the park and slid down the banister. He put his coffee cup in the dishwasher, lifted the shorts from the box, and carried them to his bedroom. His jeans slid down his muscled thighs and landed in a heap on the polished wooden floor as he solemnly tried on the mended shorts. With their new proportions they had the fit and comfort of a cross-cut saw. Paul looked down at himself and laughed until tears rolled down his cheeks. After the laughter had subsided and he was back in his jeans, he folded the shorts into the box and put them on the top shelf of his closet. "I guess I can scratch handmade gifts for Christmas," he said aloud. His smile lasted the rest of the day.

Martie listened to the tape for the umpteenth time. Paul's rich voice filled the room as he read the poetry. She sat in the middle of her bed and hugged her knees to her chest. She wanted to laugh and cry and dance and sing. She wanted to run down the street and kiss the postman who had delivered the tape. But most of all she wanted to be in the arms of the man who had recorded the love poems. "How do I love thee? Let me count the ways." His deep voice vibrated through her, and she knew that he was sharing an intimate part of himself. Through the tape she was seeing a sensitive man who recognized the beauty and music of poetry and had the ability to translate it into magic. As the tape ended, she pressed the stop button and lay back on her pillows. She closed her eyes and pretended that Paul was lying beside her, speaking the words of love as if they had been written especially for her.

*   *   *

On Thursday morning when Martie awakened and looked out her window, she was greeted by a most unexpected sight. The smile that started in her eyes spread to her lips, then widened until it swelled into laughter.

Her fence was festooned with marigolds. Peeping through every crack and crevice was a bright golden flower.

Still laughing, Martie ran toward the door, remembered that she wasn't wearing any clothes, scooted back for a robe, and flew down the stairs. "Marigolds!" she shouted with glee. "That crazy, wonderful man has decorated my fence with marigolds!"

She tugged at one of the flowers, pulling it through the fence. Masking tape dangled from the stem. Martie tucked the flower behind her ear, tape and all, and wondered how long it had taken Paul to create such an elaborate surprise. "Paul Donovan, you idiot," she whispered. "I think I'm falling in love." With light, jaunty steps, she walked back to her house. "I really must remember to patch those holes," she told herself. "This just won't do. It won't do at all." But she was smiling.

On Friday morning when Paul awakened and looked out his window, he, too, was greeted by a most unexpected sight. Grinning hugely, he erupted into a boom of laughter that bounced off the parsonage walls.

His fence looked as if it had sprouted roses. Bunches of bright red floribundas nodded in the cracks.

"My love is like a red, red rose," he quoted. "Thank you, Martie, for 'not speaking' so eloquently." Whistling he went outside and gathered the roses. One of the last flowers he plucked off the fence had a note attached: "This is positively my last communication with you, since I am still in the process of forgetting you forever and ever. Tomorrow I'm patching this fence." He put the roses in a jelly glass and set them in the middle of his kitchen table, and then he got into his reliable brown Ford and drove to the hardware store.

Martie pounded the nail home and reached behind her back for another. Her hand came up empty. "Baby, you're a big help," she scolded her unpenitent pet. "This is the third time you've stolen my sack of nails. How do you expect me to ever finish patching this fence?" She found the sack under the rosebush and continued her lopsided carpentry.

The noonday sun beamed down, too hot for October, and a trickle of sweat ran down the side of her face. She pushed up her shirt-sleeves and knotted her shirttail around her midriff. "On the whole, I'd rather be in Philadelphia," she told her rambunctious puppy.

She put her hammer on the ground and sat down to rest, but her respite was soon interrupted by a thunderous banging on the other side of the fence. Jumping up, Martie put her eye to a large crack. She couldn't see a thing except the empty parsonage yard. "Paul, is that you?" she yelled, but the enthusiastic carpentry drowned out the sound of her voice.

"What is that man up to?" she muttered, and moved to another crack in the fence, but she still couldn't see a thing. Racing to the tree, she put her foot on the lowest limb and started to climb up. She had reached only the second branch when a section of the fence crashed into her yard and the

Reverend Paul Donovan strolled through the opening.

"What in the world are you doing?" she called from the tree.

"Building a gate." He picked up the section of fence and propped it against the tree.

"Why?" She looked into his upturned face and had to clutch the branches to keep from falling. In the week since she'd seen him through the fence, she had almost forgotten how incredibly good-looking he was.

"So that I won't have to walk around the block when I want to visit you."

"You're not supposed to visit me," she reminded him. "We're not speaking."

"Those were your rules, not mine." His smile made her want to wrap around him, Aristocat style, and purr. "I'm speaking and I'm visiting," he continued, not altogether unaware of his effect on her. "Call it a pastoral call if you wish."

"Oh, dear!"

"Is that good or bad?"

"Both I think."

He chuckled. "Are you going to sit in the tree all day while you decide?"

"I don't know." She wondered how she could decide anything with him standing under her tree looking so impossibly sexy. His jeans clung to his muscular thighs, and she had a sudden vision of his shorts, Medium, 32–34. It was quite possible, she thought, that the thundering of her heart could be heard all the way to Tupelo.

"If you do, you'll miss the hamburger," he told her.

She hesitated. "It's cruel to tempt a starving woman."

"And the banana split," he continued blithely,

"oozing with chocolate syrup and heaped with whipped cream."

"Paul, that's mean." As she sprang lightly from the tree, he caught her against his chest. His face was so close she could see a tiny crescent-shaped scar in his beard shadow. "I still haven't decided, you know. I'll think about it some more over the whipped cream."

His voice was husky as he pulled her closer. "I should have built that gate last Monday."

"But then I would have missed the marigolds."

"Did you like them, Martie?"

"Yes," she whispered.

"I'm glad." He rubbed his cheek against her soft hair before he lowered her feet to the ground. "We'll go in my car," he said, surprised that his mouth could speak sane and sensible words while his heart was pounding and his mind was joyriding through fantasyland. He almost tripped over the sack of nails as one particular fantasy involving Martie in her hot-pink leotard skittered through his brain.

They went to The Sledgehammer, and it was hard to tell whether the banana split or the minister claimed more of Martie's attention. When she had finished eating she patted her mouth with a napkin. "This is bribery, you know," she told him.

"Guilty." He leaned across the table and brushed her mouth with the tip of his finger. "You missed a spot."

"Yum. Good to the last drop." Impulsively she grabbed his finger and kissed the whipped cream away. Then, with his finger still in her mouth, she looked into his eyes. They were the turbulent gray of a storm-swept sea. The tightly controlled passions she saw mirrored there made Martie want to leap across the table and take him in her arms. She wanted to caress the tension out of his shoulders and croon soft love words in his ear. Reluctantly, she released his finger. "I'm sorry, Paul."

"Don't be. It was my pleasure." He wondered if The Sledgehammer had ever been the scene of a scandal. Even if it had, what he was thinking would be one for the record.

The drive back to Martie's house was quiet as they struggled with their separate passions. She invented pressing business in the house while he finished building the gate. Every ten minutes her pressing business carried her past the kitchen window, where she could look out and observe Paul. More often than not she discovered him gazing toward the house with a heart-tugging, little-boy-lost expression on his face.

In an unaccustomed burst of domesticity, she made market-basket soup, her specialty, which consisted of everything she could find in the kitchen cabinets. But the small task didn't take her mind off the man in her yard. She stood at the window while the soup bubbled in the pot, filling the kitchen with an enticing aroma. She watched the way he moved, graceful for such a large man, and the way he stopped hammering every so often to bend down and chat with Baby.

"If I can't have him, at least I can give him a send-off that he'll never forget." Somewhere inside Martie banners unfurled and trumpet fanfares sounded, and she marched out the door to the tune of her own band.

Paul looked up from his work when he heard the screen door bang open. He started to say something, and then he saw Martie's face. He couldn't decide whether she was a David going after the giant with a stone or a Goliath laughing at the stones. Either way, he thought, she spelled excitement.

She marched straight up to him and took his hands. "Come with me," she ordered, tugging him back across the yard.

"I enjoy your surprises," he said as he followed her, "but I hope this one doesn't involve another wild ride in your little red car."

"It's going to be a wild ride all right. But not in my car." She shoved open the screen door and pulled the minister into her hallway. "This is soup and good-bye." For the first time since she had commandeered him, she looked into his face. Tipping her head back, she challenged him to deny the good-bye.

"I accept the soup." His hands moved slowly up her arms, savoring the feel of her. "But not the good-bye." He gripped her shoulders and gazed fiercely into her eyes. "Never the good-bye."

"Yes, Paul," she whispered. "But before I let you go, I want to be in your arms one last time."

He pulled her hungrily to him and cradled her head against his shoulder. "Martie, Martie. How can you be so stubborn?" He caressed her hair as he talked. "For us, there is no last time."

"Yes." She rubbed her face against the soft cotton of his plaid shirt. Underneath the fabric she could feel the thundering of his heart. Her voice was muffled against his chest. "I want a kiss that will last a lifetime."

He cupped her face and lowered his mouth to hers. The kiss was fierce, hungry, as all their pent-up passions rushed to the surface. She swayed against him and circled his waist with her arms. His hands left her face and roamed down her back, massaging with an urgency that demanded a response.

She molded her hips against his and began an erotic love dance, a tantalizing imitation of forbidden pleasures. Paul's tongue plunged into her open mouth, tasting and probing in perfect rhythm with her thrusting hips.

A red blaze of heat fogged their brains, and the restraining clothes between them seemed to vaporize. Paul was vividly aware of her breasts, peaked and straining against his chest; of the sleek line of her hips and legs, soft and pliant against his arousal. His hands slipped under her shirt, glorying in the silkiness of her bare skin, and his tongue began a slow, languid assault within the velvet depths of her willing mouth.

She was liquid fire in his arms, moving restlessly, fighting for a fulfillment she knew she couldn't have. Her silver hair floated with the motions of her head, releasing the scent of summer flowers. Paul absorbed the fragrance of her, knowing that he would never again smell violets and roses without thinking of this moment.

They clung together, prolonging the exquisite torture until they were both limp with the effort of restraint. Martie leaned her damp forehead against his chest and closed her eyes. "My mistake," she whispered. "It only makes me want more."

Paul rested his chin on top of her head and rocked her in his arms. "There will be more, Martie. I promise."

On that particular Saturday, with the forgotten soup bubbling on the stove and the hall clock chiming six, he would have proposed if he'd thought there was the ghost of a chance that she would say yes. His lips caressed her hair and he sighed. Sometimes patience was a crown of thorns.

She stood quietly in his arms, memorizing the feel of him, storing the information away for the lonely hours and days and years without him. She was almost tempted to deny their differences and plunge into a courtship with him. But for once in her impulsive life she held back, ruled by caution and self-restraint. She could accept responsibility for hurting herself, but she would not be responsible for hurting this marvelous man who was holding her so tenderly.

She lifted her head. "I've changed my mind about the soup," she murmured.

"So have I." Reluctantly, he released her. "If I don't go now, I'm afraid that I never will."

"Who would know if you stayed, Paul?" she asked softly.

"I would." He caught her fiercely to his chest for one last embrace. "Good night, angel," he said, and then he was gone.

The screen door vibrated with his leavetaking, and Martie stood in the vast emptiness of her hallway fighting a lump in her throat. "I will not cry," she said aloud, but she knew that she was fooling herself. Two glistening tears were already streaming down her cheeks. "What's the matter with me?" she cried, dashing the tears away with the back of her hand. "First I tell myself that I don't want to hurt him, and then I try to tempt him. On top of that, I'm talking to myself." She picked up a pillow from the hall settee and flung it against the wall. "Why? Why does he have to be a minister?"

The only response was the soup boiling over in the kitchen.

After she had cleaned up the mess and fed the pets and taken her bath, she tried to lose herself in an Agatha Christie mystery; but of course it was useless. With a sigh she closed the book and walked to her bedroom window. Somewhere behind the darkened fence was the parsonage, and inside that parsonage was a man who had invaded her life. A man who wouldn't go away. He clung to her thoughts as tenaciously as he clung to her life.

What was he doing? she wondered. Was he wishing that he had stayed? She paced beside the window until the hall clock chimed midnight.

Letting her silk robe drop to the floor, Martie slid between the sheets. "Tomorrow I'll put him out of my mind," she promised herself. She gave her pillows a mighty whack and tried to fall asleep.

She sat in the back row of pews and tried to be as inconspicuous as possible. Heaven only knew why she had come. She had tried to stay away; all day long she had ignored the church chimes and the tugging of her heart. But finally she had given in. Just one last glimpse of him, she had told herself. After all, she had never even heard him preach. Maybe he would be one of those pulpit-pounding, hellfire-and-damnation preachers who would make her want to leave and never see him again. She sat on the pew rationalizing as the choir filed into the loft.

A few friendly glances were cast toward her, and there were rustlings and whisperings all around. Suddenly an expectant hush fell over the crowd as the Reverend Paul Donovan stepped into the pulpit. His rich voice filled every corner of the small country church as he read the scriptures. Martie glanced around at the rapt, upturned faces of the Sunday night worshipers. There were farmers in clean, starched overalls and businessmen in three-piece suits. Good country women in plain navy dresses and pillbox hats held the hands of bright-eyed kids with freshly scrubbed faces and slicked-down hair. Stooped grandfathers with sparse white hair shared their Bibles with gangly-legged teenage grandsons. Adolescent girls with bright red lipstick and layers of makeup covering their fresh crop of pimples covertly watched their teen-age sweethearts.

Martie's eyes were drawn back toward the pulpit. She felt the strong current flowing between Paul and his parishioners. It was more than the hyp-notic beauty of his voice and the warm sincerity of his clear gray eyes. They were bound by a common purpose, a mutual seeking for the peace and strength and joy that comes through faith. She closed her eyes as Paul's compelling words swept over her, and she knew that nothing must ever separate him from his work.

Although she loved to sing, she didn't join in the final hymn. She had already determined to make a hasty exit before Paul spotted her. After the bene-diction she tried to blend in with the homeward-bound crowd, but Paul had seen her and was rapidly working his way toward the back of the sanctuary.

She had almost gained the door when a cheerful voice hailed her. "Martie! Wait!" Jolene sprinted up the side aisle and stood before her. "I saw you from the choir loft. Gosh, I thought you were going to leave before I could catch you." She took Martie's elbow and propelled her back into the church. "I meant to talk to you about the children's program last Tuesday, but it slipped my mind." She stopped talking long enough to signal frantically to Paul. "Look who I've found," she called to him.

Paul extracted himself from the crowd and joined them. "And none too soon," he remarked, beaming at Martie. "I think you've just rescued Jolene from a desperate situation."

Lightning jolted through Martie's body and thunder crashed in her ears. If Paul felt the electri-cal storm, he certainly didn't show it, she thought. How could he be talking about desperate situa-tions while she was being electrocuted? Why had she come here, and how much longer could she endure this storm without touching him?

"Desperate?" Jolene echoed plaintively. "Why, I'm positively frantic." She ran a hand through her mop of brown curls. "The play scripts arrived last week and Miss Sudie, who usually directs the Halloween pageant, has come down with flu. If Paul hadn't reminded me about you last Sunday . . . the children would have been so disappointed. Oh, my! You're a blessing in disguise."

"I haven't done anything," Martie replied. She was having a hard time following Jolene's breathless conversation, since her mind was busy memorizing every detail of Paul in his robe and clerical collar.

"But you're going to. Wait right here while I run and get the script." Jolene dashed down the aisle before Martie could say that she had no intention of ever returning to Paul's church, let alone getting involved with a Halloween pageant.

The church was empty now except for the two of them. "I'm glad you came, Martie," Paul said, taking her hand.

"It doesn't mean I've changed my mind, Paul."

"I know. But still, I'm glad. So is Jolene. I told her about your work with children in the day-care center."

Her hand nestled in his, and she felt his strength flowing into her. "I can't let the children down, can I?"

"No indeed." He smiled.

"I do love pageants!"

"I'm sure you do."

"And Halloween is just around the corner."

"It's practically here already," he agreed.

Martie's eyes sparkled as she began to anticipate the pageant. "What is the play?"

"Daniel in the Lion's Den."

She smiled with delight. "Good. We can have costumes . . . mop heads for lions' manes and red ribbons for their tails. I can even make a robe for Daniel."

"Perhaps Mrs. Pingham can help you with the sewing," he suggested, his eyes twinkling.

Martie shot him an impish grin. "You didn't like the shorts."

"I loved everything about them. Especially the lopsided leg and the heart-shaped box."

They stood in the chapel laughing, unaware that their hands were still clasped. And at that moment, Jolene walked into the back of the church. Seeing them together that way, so intent on each other, their faces shining with where-have-you-been-all-my-life joy, she laid the script on a table and made a discreet exit.

Six

Paul stood in the shadows at the back of the fellowship hall and watched Martie work. He thought
she resembled an exotic flower moving about the
small stage in her ruffled, multicolored gypsy
dress. Taking his pipe from his pocket, he eased
into a folding chair and studied the scene before
him. She was a natural with children, he decided.
Even little Sally Pingham, who had always been too
shy to participate, was enthusiastically saying her
lines.

He puffed contentedly on his pipe as the play
progressed, and if anyone had asked him to
describe it, he would have said that it was all about
a stunning woman with a knack for imparting joy
and inciting happiness.

"That's it for tonight, children," Martie called
out ten minutes later. "Cookies are in the back,
and I'll see all of you here tomorrow night."
Smiling, she took two of the chubby hands that

were thrust at her and started toward the back of the fellowship hall.

"You were wonderful."

Martie stopped as Paul's magical voice spoke from the shadows. She sent her hungry charges ahead to the kitchen. "I didn't know we had an audience," she said, turning to face him.

"I was doing some work in my office," he explained. "I thought I'd drop by and take you home."

"No thanks. It was such a pretty evening that I walked."

"So did I." He smiled. "I believe we're going the same way. We might as well go there together."

"You don't give up, do you?"

"No."

Keeping her eyes on the spiral of smoke that wafted about his head, she pondered the situation for a moment. She had known, of course, that she would see Paul while she directed the play. There was no way to avoid it. She had also known that each time she saw him she would remember the kiss they had exchanged in her back hallway. Perhaps it was best this way. Maybe if she saw him every evening, he would lose some of his appeal. Maybe she would discover that what she felt for him was merely a passing fancy rather than something akin to love. "I suppose it would look funny if we walked on opposite sides of the street," she conceded.

"People would probably talk."

"Heaven forbid! You don't mind waiting until the mothers pick up the children?"

"For you, angel, I would wait forever."

She decided not to even think about that remark. "Have a cookie while you wait."

"Did you make them?" he asked.

"Yes."

"I hope they're chocolate chip."

"Poppy seed."

He sighed. "I might have guessed."

As it turned out Paul ate more poppy-seed cookies than Skeeter, who, according to his contemporaries, had a bottomless pit for a stomach. After all the children had gone, Paul and Martie walked home in the twilight.

He took her hand as they started down the sidewalk. "In case you fall," he said.

And knowing that she was more agile than a monkey, she nestled her hand in his. Her step was jaunty, keeping time to the carousel music in her head, and rather than losing his appeal, Paul Donovan worked his way even more deeply into her heart. "I love holding hands," she said, sighing happily. "There's something so wonderfully romantic about it."

Paul lifted her hands to his lips and planted a gentle kiss on her palm. "I'll remember that," he murmured. He thought his heart would burst with love for this spontaneous woman, and he longed to take her in his arms and shout that love from the church steeple.

The kiss ignited Christmas sparklers in her body. "Not just with you, of course," she added hastily, anxious to correct any mistaken impression her words might have given him. "I love holding hands with everybody, even the postman. There's something friendly about touching, don't you think?"

He felt the fence go up between them and knew that he would have to cut another gate. "I would like to explore the difference between friendly touches and romantic touches," he replied softly.

Her mind returned to their wild embrace in her hallway. She had already explored that difference, and it was far too hot for her to handle. "If we do any more exploration, I'm afraid that I will start a scandal. I'm not as strong as you are, and besides that, I can't take refuge behind a black robe and a clerical collar."

Paul's hand tightened on hers, and he walked in silence until they came to the gate that separated their houses. Then he gripped her shoulders, forcing her to look up at him. "Ministry is a choice, Martie, not a refuge," he said, holding her gaze with his.

"I shouldn't have said that. I'm sorry, Paul."

"Don't be. You've always been candid with me. That's one of the things I like about you." He pulled her into his arms and cradled her head against his shoulder. "You keep erecting barriers where there should be none. Let it go, angel. Forget my profession and just let there be the two of us."

"I can't, Paul." She nudged her head against his shoulder, inhaling the tobacco fragrance that clung to his shirt. "I know myself too well." Tipping her head back, she flashed him an impish grin. "And if you don't let go, I'm liable to do something scandalous right here in the parsonage yard. In the public view, as Miss Beulah would say."

He released her and swung the new gate back on its hinges. "Until another time, Martie."

"Never, Paul."

He stood in the gateway until she had disappeared into her house.

Walks home together after pageant rehearsal became a nightly ritual for them, but there were no repeat performances of serious conversations and near dangerous embraces. Paul patiently respected the fence Martie had erected between them, and she unwillingly fell in love.

On Friday night it was she who stood in the gateway watching him walk back toward the parsonage. At the realization that tomorrow was Saturday, with no rehearsals and no walks home in the twilight, she was overcome by a sense of loneliness. She wanted to run after him and say, "I'll change. I'll be proper and suitable and conventional. I'll fry chicken and retire my baseball bat. I'll even give up juke music and climbing trees. I'll do anything just to be in your arms." But she didn't run after him and she didn't say those things. She could never change—not really. And even if she did, it would only be temporary. She had to be true to herself, and so did he. The gate squeaked on its tight hinges as she swung it shut and went into her own backyard.

Martie held up the shorts and giggled. She hadn't meant to buy them. She had been browsing through Michael's Department Store looking for a birthday gift for her dad when she'd spotted them. They were holdovers from Valentine's Day, the clerk had said. A marvelous pair of white shorts, Medium, 32–34, decorated with bright red hearts.

She tossed the shorts onto her bed. Of course, she couldn't give them to Paul, she told herself; it was absolutely out of the question. Maybe the purple socks, but not the shorts with red hearts. She took the socks out of the bag and examined them. They had been an impulse, too. Well, after all, Baby had mutilated his purple socks. It was the least she could do.

She put the socks back in the bag and went downstairs to create a sensational yogurt-and-tangerine shake. She sat beside the window, sipping her shake and looking out at the shadows deepening across her yard. The really sensible thing to do would be to put the gifts into a bottom drawer of her dressing table and forget about them. But then she would miss seeing Paul's smile and hearing his laughter when he opened the package. Besides, she was hardly ever sensible.

She sat at the table, arguing with herself. What she needed was a brilliant plan, one that would allow her to deliver the gifts casually as if Paul had not been uppermost in her mind for days and days. Plucking a piece of tangerine from her yogurt shake, she popped it into her mouth. She needed to be both casual and removed, she decided, out of touching distance.

Suddenly she sat up straight. The tree! Why hadn't she thought of it sooner?

Martie flew up the stairs and rummaged through her closet for wrapping paper. Frosty the Snowman would have to do. Heck, she would sing "Jingle Bells" when she delivered the gift. She wrapped the socks, changed her mind, tore off the tape, and added the shorts. It would be foolish to leave them on the bed, she rationalized. She certainly couldn't wear them, and who else did she know who wore mediums? It was only fair that Paul have the shorts with the valentines. After all, Baby had torn up his raggedy old blue ones.

Her turquoise bracelets jingled as she tied her denim western skirt between her legs. Forgetting that her cowboy hat was still on her head, she bounded down the stairs, out the door, and across the yard to her tree.

Her cowboy boots dangled from the limb as she sat forlornly in the tree and looked at the empty yard. Paul was not outside enjoying the twilight. He wasn't even home; his car was gone.

Disappointed, she started to inch back across the limb, but the tree had other ideas. Her skirt was caught in one of the branches. She reached to pull it loose, and the gift tumbled to the ground.

"I'm not sure whether it's Santa Claus or the Lone Ranger." Paul picked up the gift and smiled up at her.

The minute she saw him, "casual" flew out the window. "Paul!" she cried happily. "I thought you weren't home."

"My trusty brown Ford is in the garage. The mechanic gave me a lift home." His smile widened. "Are you coming down or are you being Baby's messenger again?"

"Neither. I'm caught." Looking down into his quicksilver-gray eyes and hearing his deep, melodious voice, Martie abandoned her "not touching" resolution. Just one more time, she told herself. She had to be in his arms just one more time. "I think if I jump, the tree will let go."

"Wait, Martie! . . ."

But it was already too late. The tree didn't let go; it held tighter, and a great tearing sound accompanied her descent to the ground. Paul tried to catch her, but the jump had been too unexpected and he wasn't prepared. She glanced off his chest and they both crashed into the marigold bed.

His arms wrapped around her as they rolled in the dirt. Her cowboy hat and the Christmas-wrapped gift skittered across the ground, forgotten. With legs entangled and lips only a kiss away, Paul and Martie had thoughts only for each other. Skyrockets exploded inside them as their bodies made intimate contact in the dirt. Her silk-clad hip, exposed through the torn skirt, pressed against his groin.

A half-strangled sound escaped his lips as he raised himself to his knees and looked down at her. "Are you all right?"

"Yes," she said, but her mind was screaming *No!* She would never be all right until she had Paul. All of him—not just a hungry embrace in a hallway or an intimate tumble in the dirt, but every glorious inch of him, without restrictions.

He scooped her into his arms and carried her inside the parsonage. "Let's brush away all that dirt," he said, but what he meant was "Let's get inside before I lose control of the situation."

Still keeping his arm around her waist, he set her down beside the kitchen sink and reached for a towel, turning on the water with one hand. "This will only take a minute."

"I hope it takes a year."

"Martie?" He turned and saw her eyes, naked with desire and dark as the velvet throat of pansies.

The towel dropped to the floor and the water gurgled down the sink drain as he pulled her into his arms. His hands tangled in her hair, and he crushed her against his chest as if he would never let go. They stood this way for a moment, swaying to the combined rhythms of their runaway hearts.

In slow motion they inched apart so that their lips could meet. The kiss was a blending of drugged sweetness and honeyed desire. It was a Fourth of July parade and a homecoming celebration. It was passion and joy and burning need. And it was perfection because they loved.

Trapped in their mistaken notions of barriers and suitability, they let their bodies speak what they dared not. He pressed her hips against his, marveling at how right it felt, while his tongue plied its urgent message inside her mouth. She writhed in his arms, moist and open with undisguised longing. The fever that possessed them raged unchecked, and they gasped with the heat of it.

His mouth moved away from her love-pouted lips and seared down the side of her neck. She threw back her head to accommodate his questing mouth, and her hair fanned out in a bright curtain against his arms. Her pulse tore at her throat as one of Paul's hands moved inside her open-necked shirt to cup a taut breast. A thousand stars burst inside her at his touch, and she was Aphrodite and Earth Mother rolled into one.

And when there was nowhere else to go except the final fulfillment, Paul gently released her. "I think I took care of all the dirt." His breathing was still ragged and his smile was lopsided.

Martie lifted her hair away from her flushed face. "I don't know how this keeps happening," she whispered. "It's not supposed to."

"We can't prevent it, angel."

"We must. I won't play Delilah to your Samson."

"My career and my professional reputation are my responsibility, Martie, not yours."

"Then why do I feel like a temptress?" she asked.

"Perhaps it's because you think of me only as a minister and not a man."

She waved her hands in the air, setting her bracelets to jingling. "I can't think of all that right now. I . . ." She paused and a small grin lit her face. "The water's still running."

"I beg your pardon."

"You forgot to turn off the faucet."

Paul grinned sheepishly as he twisted the faucet handle. "You made me forget."

"So did you."

"What?"

"Make me forget . . . I brought you a present."

"The Christmas package?" he asked.

"Call it a going-away gift."

"I'm not going anywhere, angel. Are you?"

"Yes. I'm going across the fence and out of your life." She cocked her head to one side in thought. "At least, after Halloween I'm going out of your life. Good-bye, Paul." It was one of her most flamboyant exits, mainly because of the great tear in the back of her skirt.

Paul thought he was just about under control until he saw the long, lovely tanned legs and firm bottom encased in a black silk teddy. As the screen door banged behind her, he rushed to the sink, turned on the faucet, and stuck his face under the cool water.

Martie shut her mind to everything until she was across the parsonage yard, through the gate, and back in her own house. And then it all came pouring over her—Paul and the marigold bed and Baby's shenanigans and the whipped cream and the gate. But most of all the kisses. She leaned her forehead against the cool windowpane and looked back toward the parsonage. There was no use denying it, she thought. She was in love with the Reverend Paul Donovan. She, Martie Fleming, fun-time honky-tonk girl, had fallen for Pontotoc's pillar of faith and strength, the spiritual leader of Faith Church. If there were only the two of them, perhaps the love might work. But there were also the Miss Beulahs and the Essie Maes, not only in this town, but in every other town that Paul would serve. There were the people who never looked beyond appearances, people whose world was black and white with no shades of gray, people who saw and judged.

She banged her fist against the kitchen table, scraping the skin on a knuckle. Damn! Why was life so unfair? Why couldn't she have moved next door to a plumber?

She went upstairs, removed her torn clothes, showered off all the dirt, and went to bed. But she didn't sleep. She thought she might never sleep again as long as she lived.

* * *

A loud clamoring at her back door awakened Martie. Her usual bounce was missing as she climbed out of bed, and she was halfway to the bedroom door before she remembered that she didn't have on a stitch of clothes. She reached for her robe and grasped emptiness. "I'm coming," she called as she walked back to the bed and pulled off the sheet. Knotting it just above her breasts, she swept out the door, trailing four feet of red-and-white-striped percale.

"You're not dressed," Paul said when she opened the door. Seeing her tanned shoulders and the swell of breasts above the sheet, he almost forgot why he had come.

"I wasn't counting on a tea party at this hour," Martie replied, struggling to keep from wrapping him in her sheet and whisking him up to her bedroom. "Did you come to return the gift?"

"No. I came to hitch a ride to church." He grinned. "I'm wearing the gift."

"The socks or the shorts?" she asked curiously.

"Both."

"I wish I could see."

"So do I."

They stood in the doorway in the wash of early morning sun and almost forgot about all the reasons they couldn't be together. His knuckles turned white on the door frame, and her hand clung desperately to the door handle as they fought the urge to embrace and never let go.

Martie was the first to break the silence. "I'm not going to church this morning," she said, averting her gaze from his. "I would be going for all the wrong reasons, and I don't want to torture myself by looking at something I can't have."

"All we need is time, Martie."

"Time wouldn't change a thing. I would still be me and you would still be you." She jerked her head toward the kitchen. "Take my car. The keys are on the kitchen counter."

He reached out and gently traced the stubborn line of her jaw with his index finger. "I'll be out of town next week at a ministers' conference, but I'll be back for the Halloween festival. When I get back, we'll talk."

"Go, Paul, before I change my mind."

"About the car?" he asked.

"No. About wrapping you in this sheet and taking you upstairs."

He left. But not before he had wrestled with temptation.

Miss Beulah Grady was the first to see the minister emerge from the bright red Thunderbird. "As I live and breathe!" The purple pansies on her dress did the cha-cha as she heaved across the churchyard to Essie Mae. "Did you see that?" she cried, trying to catch her breath. "She's got the preacher riding in that heathen car!"

"Lord, Beuler!" Essie Mae's mouth watered as she imagined the scandalous things that could happen in a heathen car. "The next thing you know she'll have him wearing red neckties."

Martie smiled as she affixed manes to her "lions." Sally's cat and Jim's dog cooperated beautifully, but Skeeter's goat didn't want to be a lion. "Hold him, Skeeter," she instructed the twelve-year-old, "while I get this mane on."

"Gee, Miss Fleming. You're the neatest director we ever had, letting us use our pets in the pageant." Skeeter thought his heart would burst with admiration. When the idea of using pets as lions had first come up, he hadn't been sure Miss Fleming would let him use Billy. But she'd been a real sport about it. She was even letting Martha Sue use her goldfish. Personally, he thought the mane and tail on the goldfish bowl looked funny, but it made Martha Sue happy.

"Thanks, Skeeter. Now, you keep a tight rein on Billy. If our lions behave, perhaps they can be sheep in the Christmas pageant."

"Golly, Miss Fleming!" Skeeter cried, eyes wide. "Will you direct the Christmas pageant, too?"

"Well, I—"

"Don't you know anything, silly?" Francine interrupted. "My mama says the preacher's got eyes for Miss Fleming. Preachers' wives *always* direct the pageants." Having set the record straight on how things were done in the church, Francine turned to her idol. "My Siamese keeps trying to get into Martha Sue's fishbowl, Miss Fleming. He hasn't had any dinner yet."

If Francine's gossip hadn't been enough to give Martie's stomach butterflies, this latest bit of information did. In her usual burst of hindsight, she reflected that perhaps the lions hadn't been such a good idea after all. "When we get onstage," she told Francine, "be sure that cat is on the opposite side from the goldfish."

"What about Sally's cat?" Francine asked.

"Hers, too." Martie busied herself getting the children ready for the pageant, hoping the activity would keep her mind off Francine's remark. Unfortunately, the ploy didn't work. Her head spun with the phrase "preacher's wife" until she thought she would explode with the wonder and the terror of it all.

Nervously she glanced at her watch. She hadn't been this scared facing bulls in Tijuana. Tonight was more than a Halloween pageant: it was her debut, a test of her suitability. Outside, she could hear laughter and excited conversation as women put their cakes on display for the upcoming cake auction and men set up booths for "go fishing" and fortune-telling. As she listened, she recognized Paul's deep, rich voice, and her knees went weak. How could she keep from rushing into his arms when she saw him? If it hadn't been for pageant rehearsals, this past week would have been the longest in her life. The time away from him had intensified her conviction that she loved him.

Jolene tapped at the dressing room door and called, "We're ready, Martie."

"Thanks, Jolene." Taking a deep breath, she sent King Darius and his court onstage.

Holding her prompting book, Martie stood in the darkened wings and watched her production. Skeeter, a natural-born ham, was in his element, strutting around in his towel robes and cardboard crown. There was a hush over the audience as the children gave lively new meaning to the story of Daniel in the lions' den. When the curtain rang down on the first act, the audience cheered and applauded.

Martie hugged her amateur actors. "You were all wonderful!" she cried. "Now, let's get these lions onstage for the second act."

There was a collective gasp from the audience as the curtain rang up and the motley crew of lions came into view. Faith Church had never seen such a pageant as this. The murmur of excitement faded as Daniel was cast into the pit and started to say his lines. Little Bobby Wayne had won a few oration contests, and he made himself heard, even over the titters that erupted in the back of the hall when one of the lions had to scratch fleas.

Martie congratulated herself on the success of her production as she sent the angel in to shut the lions' mouths. Sally's bedsheet robe trailed behind her, and she held her candle aloft as she walked onstage. Only a slight trembling in her voice betrayed her nervousness.

"I command you to be shut." Sally repeated the phrase three times as she passed in front of the goldfish bowl and two beagles. Her confidence flagged when Francine's Siamese hissed at her, and by the time she got to Bobby Wayne's bulldog, her knees were shaking. When the bulldog growled, she dropped her candle and fled in terror.

"Sally, wait!" Martie called, but it was too late. She watched in horror as the lighted candle rolled under the goat's tail.

Billy took exception. With a great "Baa," he lowered his head and charged at the biggest target in the room . . . Miss Beulah.

Seeing the mad goat jump off the stage and stampede her way, Miss Beulah climbed on top of her chair and yelled, "Saints preserve us!" The chair was not meant to endure such treatment. It died a painful, splintering death, and Miss Beulah rolled across the floor with the goat close behind.

Martie stood hypnotized, watching the pandemonium from her vantage point on the stage. She saw Paul collar the goat just in time to save Miss Beulah, but before she could breathe a sigh of relief she saw movement on the stage.

Francine's Siamese was taking advantage of the situation to dive at Martha Sue's goldfish, and the beagles thought the chase meant rabbits. Sounding their bugle calls, they entered the hunt. One of them ran through Essie Mae's legs, knocking her onto the lap of the astonished postman, and the other ran under the table of desserts at the back of the room. He bumped the table leg, sending a chocolate-cream pie into flight. The airborne pie landed in Sam's lap.

"I've been wanting to do this for years," Sam

said. Grabbing a lemon meringue pie, she sailed it across the topsy-turvy room into the livid face of Miss Beulah.

Martie jumped off the stage and entered the melee. The bulldog brushed past her leg in pursuit of a cat, another pie flew through the air and sprayed whipped cream onto her hair, and somebody screamed into her ear that Judgment Day had come. She collared dogs and grabbed cats, pulling them out of the pandemonium and giving them to their gleeful owners.

Sally tugged at her skirt and looked up with tearful eyes. "I didn't even get to do the third act," she wailed.

Martie gave her a swift hug. "The play is over, darling. Maybe you can be an angel again at Christmastime." She gave the small girl a last reassuring pat. "You can take your cat and go home now," she said gently, then straightened up and found herself face to face with Paul. He winked at her and continued on his way, calmly restoring order to the chaos.

When the dust had settled and the excited crowd had gone home, Paul and Martie stood among the chocolate icing and overturned chairs and looked at each other.

"I don't know whether to laugh or cry," Martie said.

"It was a memorable Halloween," Paul said.

"I think Miss Beulah was mad about the goat." Her mouth began to curve upward into a smile.

"I think that's the understatement of the year." Paul began to chuckle and then to laugh, and soon his laughter erupted into a full-fledged roar. "You should have seen her face when that goat almost tagged her bloomers."

They collapsed into the rubble, laughing until tears streamed down their cheeks.

A clatter of hoofbeats caught their attention as Skeeter and his goat emerged from behind the stage curtain. "We came back to tell you that this has been the most fun we've ever had at Halloween," he announced happily, his face covered with chocolate and whipped cream.

"Maybe we can get Miss Fleming to do the pageant again next year," Paul told him, "but without the chase and the pie fight."

Skeeter beamed. "That would be swell, Reverend Donovan." He left the stage, leading Billy on a tether.

Paul captured Martie's hand and lifted it to his lips. "How does that sound to Miss Fleming?"

"Like an impossible pipe dream, Reverend Donovan."

Seven

Paul looked up from the sermon he was preparing. He had expected visitors, but not this soon. Miss Beulah had wasted no time, he thought as he mentally girded himself for the skirmish.

His face betrayed no emotion as he came from behind his desk, shook hands with Victor Cranston, and showed Miss Beulah and Essie Mae to their chairs. "What can I do for you this morning?" he asked.

"I should think you would know that as well as anybody." Miss Beulah's lips were so pursed that her words all came out with rounded vowels. "I didn't sleep a wink last night for fear that goat would come after me. And on top of that, *she* played that honky-tonk music until the Lord knows when. She's a sin and disgrace to our little community. A dis-*grace*." She stopped for breath and fanned herself with her fat hands.

Essie Mae leaned over and patted her shoulder.

"Lord, Beuler!" she said sympathetically. "Don't get yourself so worked up. You're liable to have a prostration attack."

Paul held himself in check throughout the speech. "Miss Beulah, I am well aware that the pageant last night got out of hand," he began quietly, "but I will not tolerate a personal attack against Martie Fleming. Perhaps she made an error in judgment in using the animals, but her intentions were good. I will listen to your grievances as long as you confine them to the issue."

Victor Cranston spoke up. "The issue, Reverend Donovan, is Miss Fleming. We believe she is a bad influence on the children and should be removed from the children's department."

"A bad influence, my eye!" Miss Beulah chimed in. "She's a Jezebel. Flashing that gaudy jewelry, wearing those outlandish clothes. And that car! Lord, I won't even mention that car! Why, I said to Essie Mae, I said—"

"Miss Beulah!" Paul's rebuke was sharper than he meant it to be, but he could stand no more slurs against his beloved Martie. "Nobody in this room has a right to judge. You've all taken note of Miss Fleming's clothes and her car, but have you actually seen her work with the children? Have you seen the warmth and generosity and compassion she has for them? Have you seen her inspire shy little Sally Pingham to take a speaking part in the pageant? Did you know that the Raiford twins are now coming to Faith Church because of her? Have any of you taken the time to get to know Miss Fleming, or have you tried and convicted her on first impressions?"

There was a stunned silence following his impassioned defense of Martie. One by one the self-appointed, self-righteous grievance committee rose from their chairs.

"We'll give this some further consideration, Reverend," Victor Cranston mumbled.

The pink peonies on Miss Beulah's dress trembled as she talked. "Perhaps we were a mite hasty. That goat had me so upset. . . . Oh, my! I think I'll go to the drugstore for some lemonade." She sprang from her chair with surprising alacrity considering her vast bulk. "Are you coming, Essie Mae?"

"Wild horses couldn't keep me away. I think the postman stops there about this time every morning." Thinking how that sounded, Essie Mae hastily added, "I want to ask him about air mail."

After the three of them had departed, Paul dropped to his knees and had a long conference with his Master about tolerance and patience.

Martie dismissed her Jazzercise class and turned off the record. Sam and Jolene made no pretense of leaving. Draping towels around their perspiring necks, Jolene plopped into a chair and Sam sat cross-legged on the floor.

"Let's talk about last night, Martie," Jolene said.

Martie sat on the floor and stretched out her legs. "It was a disaster, huh?"

Jolene smiled. "Not entirely."

Sam chimed in, "Heck, I thought it was fun."

Jolene turned to her. "You thought the picnic was fun the year Miss Beulah fell into the pond."

"She's a busybody," Sam said.

Martie held up her hands. "All right, you guys. Quit kidding around and lay it on the line. I'm not suitable for the children's department and I hereby resign."

"Over my dead body!" Jolene said. "You've breathed life into that department. But let's not have any more pageants with real animals until the storm dies down."

"You can't quit," Sam told her. "Paul Donovan would be crushed. He's in love with you."

Martie tried to hide the rush of pleasure that statement brought by wiping her face with her towel. "Why don't we leave Paul out of this?" she suggested. "The fact is, I've created a stir in the church, and I'm not sure it would be wise for me to continue as children's director. I love the children, but I want what's best for them."

"You're the best for them," Jolene said.

"No doubt about it," Sam agreed.

Martie laughed. "You two are real friends. I wish everybody would feel that way. Let me give this some more thought."

Impulsively, Sam reached over and hugged her. "We're going to pester you until you say you'll stay."

"I'll count on it." Martie escorted her friends to the door and stood waving as they drove off in Sam's battered pickup truck.

After they had gone, she changed into jeans and a bright blue sweater and went outside to do some yard work. She sat on her heels beside a bed of chrysanthemums and spaded the weeds. Digging in the earth always had a calming effect on her, and heaven knew she needed calming down today. She imagined that Paul was also seeking solace in activity. If nothing else, the Halloween pageant should have convinced him that she didn't fit into a conservative life-style.

She attacked a weed with such vigor that she broke a fingernail. Good, she thought. Maybe she could transfer the pain in her heart to her finger. She had never dreamed that giving up Paul would be this hard. But she must! He was probably going through torture today because of her shenanigans last night. She hadn't meant to cause such a ruckus; it was simply a part of her nature. As a matter of fact, if she hadn't been worried about the trouble she'd caused for the man she loved, she would have been chuckling over the whole thing.

Baby trotted over and dropped a faded pink rubber ball behind her back. Martie turned around and leaned her head on her pet's soft golden fur. "Tell me how to handle heartbreak, Baby," she murmured. "I've never been in love before."

Baby happily wagged her tail in the mistaken belief that she was the center of her mistress's universe.

Martie handled heartbreak by staying so busy that she didn't have time to think. She played ball with Baby and cleaned kitchen cabinets and baked poppy-seed cookies. Every time a certain gray-eyed man popped into her thoughts, she went into a flurry of activity that would have made the faint-hearted dizzy just watching.

A few blocks away in the pastor's study, Paul took the opposite approach to the problem. Instead of pushing it away, he studied it from all angles. He believed that in time Martie's detractors would begin to appreciate all the wonderful qualities that he saw in her. That part of the problem would work itself out. The major hurdle he had to overcome right now was the one Martie herself manufactured. He could almost see her mind magnifying last night's incidents and putting another fence between them. He knew that if he let her use the Halloween pageant as an excuse to avoid him, he would surely lose her. The situation called for a large dose of the tenacity he had confessed to having.

Having decided upon his course of action, he finished his work and headed straight for Martie's house just as the sun was disappearing. He parked his car and walked to her back door. Her loud, jazzy music assaulted his ears and he smiled. Without knocking, he pushed open the screen door and went inside. Aristocat and Baby, who were by now accustomed to his sudden appearances, escorted him down the hall to Martie's exercise room. He sat in one of the chairs against the wall and drank in the sight of her. Her wonderful silver hair was caught in a scarlet ribbon high on her head and cascaded down in bright confusion. The red leotard was cut high on the sides and low in the front, revealing enough smooth, tanned skin to make Paul's heart do flip-flops. He was so entranced that he forgot to take out his pipe.

Unaware of his presence, Martie gyrated to the beat of the music, hoping to exhaust her energetic body so that she could fall asleep without another lengthy session of rationalizing her actions. She was tired of arguing with herself and impatient with complicated situations. She almost wished for the carefree days of moving around the country, doing whatever took her fancy. Almost, but not quite. She didn't want to give up her house and her yard and her flower beds, her little piece of earth. Most of all she didn't want to give up her beloved Reverend Paul Donovan. Even if he couldn't be her lover, he still made a wonderful backyard neighbor.

The dance ended with a drum cadence and a loud burst of applause. Startled, Martie spun around to see Paul sitting quietly against the wall. Without thinking, she flew across the room, arms outstretched.

Paul stood so quickly the chair crashed to the floor. His arms welcomed her trim, perspiring body.

She nuzzled her head against his shoulder. "You old honey bear!" she cried. "How long have you been sitting there?"

"Long enough to know that I can never let you go."

"Paul!" Her anguished cry was born of the realization that once again she had let her heart rule her head. Without thinking she had yielded to her natural impulse—to get as close as possible to the man she loved. She put her hands against his chest and pushed herself out of his arms. "I didn't mean to do that."

"I'm glad you did, Martie. It proves my point."

"I'm not even going to ask."

"You already know. We were meant to be together and nothing can stop us. Not anything nor anybody." He caught her shoulders and pulled her back into his arms. "Not even you."

"It won't work, Paul," she said, resting her head on his shoulder. "After last night you should know that."

He chuckled. "Last night got a little out of hand, but it was no disaster. It might even be a blessing in disguise. When word gets around, the pews will be spilling over with curious people."

"You're too good, Paul. Why aren't you chastising me for being so foolhardy? I'll bet half your congregation is in cultural shock today." She sighed. "I've given this some thought. I won't be a part of your life anymore, and I certainly won't be a part of your work. I'm nothing but trouble for you, and I'll never change."

He stood very still, and only the tensing of his jaw betrayed his conflict. "I don't want you to change," he said, tilting her chin so that she had to look up at him. "Before you go, I want to give you something." He pulled her so close that she found it hard to breathe, and then his mouth crushed hers with fierce possessiveness, dominating, demanding, taking charge in a savage kiss that ripped away barriers of any kind between them.

Martie clung to him, feeling boneless and light-headed as the embrace transported her into a starburst world of yearning flesh and heated passions. He pulled her scantily clad hips against his as his tongue took her mouth with quick, explosive thrusts. They swayed together, and the roughness of his shirt abraded her jutting nipples. Her legs would hardly support her weight when he finally released her.

"Tell me again how you're going out of my life," he demanded hoarsely.

Her voice shook as she tried to turn the situation around. "A kiss to last a lifetime, Paul?"

"No. A kiss to begin a lifetime."

"Wrong. I won't deny that I respond to your kisses, but I still haven't changed my mind about stepping out of your life."

Paul's eyes darkened. He still had one trump card, he reflected. If he knew Martie as well as he thought he did, this one should do the trick. "That's exactly what Miss Beulah wants you to do."

"Miss Beulah has nothing to do with this decision," Martie declared, frowning.

"I know that, but she'll be overjoyed to hear about it."

Her eyes blazed as she thrust out her stubborn jaw. "Has she been to see you?"

"You know that's confidential, Martie," Paul replied blandly. "I can't tell you who comes to me for counseling." He suppressed a smile as he watched her come up fighting.

"She has! I wish that goat *had* tagged her bloomers." Martie paced the floor with long, angry strides and waved her hands in the air as she talked. "She wants you to get rid of me, doesn't she? Never mind what the children want! Well, you can tell her for me that I wouldn't leave the children's department in a million years. Not even if the president of the United States asked me to."

He could no longer hold back his smile; it burst forth, a beacon of joy that lit up the room. "Does this mean that you aren't leaving?"

"You bet your britches, I'm not! Those children are *my* work, Paul. Forget about telling Miss Beulah. I'll tell her myself."

"Now that the crisis is over, I'm famished. What do you have in your refrigerator?"

"Salami and some tofu, I think."

"Wait right here, angel. I'll go home and get the cheese."

"I adore impromptu picnics. Let's eat outside under the oak tree."

They did. And while they ate, Paul reflected that for him it was a victory celebration. He could see time wearing away the edges of Martie's defensiveness. He would wait, not as patiently as he first had, but with the sure knowledge that she would someday come to him freely, unfettered by doubts and mistaken convictions.

The wind nipping around them finally drove them inside. Paul built the first fire of the season in Martie's fireplace, and she dragged out a long-handled corn popper. They burned the first batch but eventually got the hang of it.

After the popcorn was gone Paul stayed to hear the last few songs on the Ray Charles record they were playing. And then came the rain, fat droplets that splatted against the windowpane and danced on the rooftop. Martie wouldn't hear of him leaving in the rain, and he cheerfully agreed that he would probably melt if he got wet. The steady beat of the rain, the crackle of the fire, and the haunting strains of blues music set the stage for two people who skirted around their love and failed to recognize their compatibility. The fence Martie had built between them was so shaky that one puff from Paul would have blown it down, but he didn't know that. And she didn't know that the fishbowl life she had imagined for him existed primarily in her own mind.

When the fire had died to embers and the rain had become nothing more than a soft sighing of wind, Paul went home. And Martie's heart went with him.

Paul was sitting in the back of the darkened church listening to the choir practice when Martie swept down the aisle in her purple tie-dyed caftan. He saw the shock wave wash over the members of the adult choir as she made her flamboyant way to the choir loft. Making a steeple of his folded hands, he sat back to watch the action.

"Hello, everybody," Martie called, and waved, jingling her ornate copper-and-brass bracelet. "I've come to join the choir."

Paul grinned as Essie Mae hit a resounding off-key chord on the organ and Miss Beulah dropped her hymnbook on the postman's toe. Trust Martie to create a stir wherever she went, he thought.

Completely unaware of the interested observer in the back of the church, Martie mounted the steps to the choir loft, the sleeves of her caftan flowing behind her, and took her place beside an apoplectic Miss Beulah. "Since Pontotoc is going to be my permanent home," she announced, "I've decided to get involved in everything that interests me. I like to sing."

"Bravo, Martie," Paul whispered.

Buck Hunter, the choir director, who had been crowned with a coconut-cream pie at the Halloween fiasco, gave Martie a thin smile. "What do you sing?"

Paul saw the impish grin light her face as she answered, "Mostly country-western and blues. Some call it honky-tonk music. But I can sing anything. Church music, too."

Don't go too far, Martie, Paul pleaded silently. Just this once curb your impulses.

The top of Buck's bald head turned red, and he coughed behind his freckled hand. "I meant what part do you sing?"

"Alto," she replied. "Low voices are best suited for performing, you know."

Miss Beulah, who had been twitching as if she were sitting in a bed of ants, could no longer keep quiet. "You've *performed*?"

In the back of the church, Paul sent a silent prayer winging upward. He knew that tone of voice: it was the one Miss Beulah used when she was breathing down the neck of scandal.

"Oh, yes," Martie answered serenely. "Performing is a great way to meet people. I have friends all over the West." She smiled directly into Miss Beulah's mortified face. "I find that most people are good-hearted and quite likable, don't you?"

Paul nearly gave himself away by laughing aloud. He recovered in time, so that only a small strangled sound escaped his lips.

Miss Beulah fidgeted. "Why I . . . that is to say . . . and on the other hand . . ." For once in her life, she was speechless. If she had been a balloon, she would have risen slowly to the ceiling and whined around the church as the air escaped. She was, to say the least, deflated. "B-Buck," she finally stammered, "what did you say the next number was?"

"Number one fifty-three. 'Love, Mercy, and Grace.' "

"Thank you, Lord," Paul whispered as the organ boomed a chord and the choir got off to a shaky start. He relaxed, listening to the music, and suddenly he was riveted to his seat. As the choir began the chorus, Martie's distinctive, husky voice wrapped itself like velvet around the words. The beauty of her singing soared through the church, and Paul was sure that even the angels must be bending down to listen.

When choir practice ended Paul joined the singers chatting at the front of the church. He was pleased to see that feelings toward Martie had mellowed; she was the center of a laughing group, and even her outrageous costume seemed to have been forgotten.

Martie felt a delicious tingling sensation when she saw Paul. Keeping him always in sight, she chatted with first one departing group and then another until only the two of them were left.

"Well." Paul felt like a tongue-tied adolescent as he stood smiling at her.

"Well?" Martie spread her arms wide and shrugged her shoulders.

"You were wonderful." He crossed quickly to her and put an arm across her shoulders. "Let's go to my office for a cup of coffee."

"A celebration?"

"With you, everything is a celebration," he replied softly.

Paul's office was a small, book-lined cubbyhole that smelled like sandalwood because of the scented candle burning on his desk. Martie ran her hand over the book spines as Paul measured coffee into the glass coffeepot. As she had expected, the shelves contained several volumes of poetry. She pulled out a dog-eared volume of Shakespeare's sonnets.

"Would you read for me, Paul?"

"You wouldn't rather talk?"

"No."

"What would you like me to read?" he asked, leafing through the slim volume.

"You choose."

He chose "Shall I Compare Thee to a Summer's Day?" The candle burned low as Martie sat beside his desk, enthralled by the sound of his voice. When the reading was finished, she flung her arms wide in ecstasy, trailing the sleeve of her caftan across the candle. They both froze as flames licked her sleeve, igniting the caftan.

Neither of them could have related what happened next. But Miss Beulah Grady could. Unknown to them, she had come all the way back from the parking lot to have a heart-to-heart talk with the minister. Hearing voices as she neared his study, she had stopped to listen. Not to eavesdrop, of course, she had assured herself, but merely to find out who was in there and how long they might stay. Recognizing Martie's voice, she had inched closer, hoping to catch the words. Plain as day she had heard the minister tell that brazen woman she had "darling buds."

Miss Beulah's mouth went slack. For a minute she was too shocked to move, then she leaned over and put her eye to the keyhole. She had to maneuver a little to get a clear view of both of them. To her utter amazement, she saw Reverend Donovan rip Martie's caftan down the front and throw it on the floor. And that scandalous honky-tonk woman was wearing a wisp of scarlet lace held together with scarlet ribbons. Miss Beulah was agog at the amount of flesh she was showing, and every inch of it tan. She looked like something straight out of an Old West saloon. While Miss Beulah was still making that comparison she saw the Reverend Donovan's arms go around that hussy. He pulled her so close it was a wonder he didn't break her ribs. And such kissing! Miss Beulah pressed her face closer to the keyhole. She hadn't ever seen anything like that. It was a wonder they didn't swallow each other.

Sweat streamed down the side of Miss Beulah's face, ran down her neck and between her heaving bosoms. She had never felt so overheated in her life. She thought she might have a prostration attack when all this was over. The two people inside the study moved away from the door, toward the small love seat—and a good thing they did, too, because if they hadn't, she might not have been able to see what happened next. That shameless woman unbuttoned the preacher's shirt and ran her hands over his bare chest. Miss Beulah's eyes practically popped out of her head. She had never dreamed the preacher was hiding a chest like *that* under his robes. The saints have mercy! She glued her eyes still closer to the keyhole. The long-suffering door gave way under the added pressure, and Miss Beulah catapulted into the room.

For a moment the two people merely looked at their unwelcome intruder in surprise; then Paul swiftly bent down, picked up Martie's caftan, and draped it over her. "This is not what it seems, Miss Beulah," he said quietly as he moved away from Martie.

Both Miss Beulah's chins were trembling with the excitement of it all. "Reverend Donovan, in all my born days I've never witnessed anything like this. Why, I thought my eye would pop right through the keyhole!"

"You were watching us through the keyhole?" Paul asked, his voice tight.

"I saw it *all*. And I must say that I'm shocked, *shocked* at what was going on in this room. When I tell the pastor-parish relations committee what I saw—"

"Be sure to tell them that you were the first to

know," Martie broke in. She was so angry that her voice was shaking. How dare Miss Beulah spy through the keyhole! she fumed. How dare she plan to ruin Paul's career by misinterpreting what she saw! It was one thing for Miss Beulah to talk about her misdeeds, but it was another thing altogether to drag Paul into a scandal. Martie couldn't let it happen. "We're going to be married," she blurted out.

Paul sucked in his breath and Miss Beulah's mouth dropped open.

"We were going to announce it soon," Martie continued, "but now you can do that for us." She stopped and shivered. Oh, dear! Now she had done it. They would never extricate themselves from this mess.

Paul put his arm around her and drew her to his side. "We were planning to surprise everybody, Miss Beulah, but now the cat's out of the bag. By the time you see us again, we will be Reverend and Mrs. Paul Donovan. I'm counting on you to share the good news with the rest of the parishioners."

The knowledge that she was the first to know took the edge off Miss Beulah's self-righteous indignation. She swung her mountain of flesh out the door without saying good-bye. "Just wait 'til I tell Essie Mae," they heard her say as she disappeared down the hall.

Martie raised stricken eyes to Paul's face. "Oh, dear! What will we do now?"

"Get married," he said, smiling.

Eight

They had a small ceremony in the church with Jolene, Bob, and Sam as witnesses; Reverend Tom Stegall, a friend of Paul's who served a small parish in nearby Saltillo, officiated. Afterward Paul helped Martie move into the parsonage.

"You don't think it's necessary for me to sleep over there, do you?" Martie asked, looking up from the box of books she was packing. "Maybe I could just putter around the parsonage in the daytime to keep up appearances and slip quietly through the gate at night." She didn't know if she could be under the same roof with him at night without making a fool of herself. They had a paper now that made sleeping with him all nice and legal, but it didn't make a damn bit of difference. She knew that he had married her to save his career and that his scruples would keep him from consummating a marriage that was not real.

His heart turned over at the forlorn look on her

face. He wanted to take her in his arms and tell her how much he loved her. He wanted to drop down on his knees and take her hand and tell her that he had meant every word of his wedding vows. He wanted to carry her over the threshold and into his bedroom and make her his wife in every sense of the word. But he couldn't do any of those things. He knew that she had married him out of unselfish generosity. She had made it perfectly clear that she would never willingly choose the conventional life of a minister's wife. As much as he wanted to make love to her, as much as he wanted to bind her to him with passion, he would never take unfair advantage of her.

He leaned against the bookshelf and took out his pipe, small consolation for the frustration he was feeling. While he was filling his pipe, he carefully considered his answer. He wanted to reassure her without closing the door to other possibilities. Lifting the pipe to his mouth, he took a slow draw. He was determined to move heaven and earth so that someday they would truly be man and wife. But he was a patient man. For now, he would wait. "I'm afraid you have to move in full-time," he replied slowly. "But don't worry. The parsonage has more than one bedroom. And I promise not to bite."

"I'm scared that I'm the one who will bite." Seeing the gleam in his eyes, she hastened to steer the conversation toward safer topics. "I've never had a housemate. I'm not sure you'll be able to stand me. I get up early to jog and I play my music loud and I leave wet towels on the bathroom floor."

"You also eat cow food." He smiled at her. "I'll take these boxes across while you pack your clothes."

She watched until he was out the door and then she kicked a box. Dammit! she raged. Why didn't he know that she loved him? The big galoot! Did she have to hang a sign around her neck? She raced upstairs and began slinging her lingerie into a suitcase. A lot of good it did to own sexy under-things. That thick-headed, oversized, wonderful, remarkable, marvelous, gorgeous man would never even see them. She pressed her hands to her hot face. She wanted to just march right into the parsonage and shout, "I love you, dammit! I've always loved you and I always will." But she couldn't do that. It was bad enough that he was saddled with the most unsuitable minister's wife the world had ever seen. She wouldn't complicate matters by hanging around his neck like an albatross.

She dragged another suitcase from her closet. She didn't know whether to pack all of her clothes or just a few. She decided on a few. Maybe Paul would think of a way out, and she could move to Outer Mongolia to get over her heartbreak.

She heard him whistling as he came up the stairs. She sat on her suitcase to snap the lock, wishing there were something to whistle about. The lid refused to close. She was still sitting on the bulging suitcase, struggling with the lock, when Paul came in.

"Don't tell me you're trying to hitch a ride to the parsonage on your suitcase. I don't know if I'm up to that, ma'am." He leaned in the doorway, aching to devour her.

She batted her eyelashes at him. "Why, honey-pot, I married you for your muscles. You're not going to disappoint me, are you?"

"No, indeed." He strode across the room and scooped her up, suitcase and all.

She laced her arms around his neck to keep from toppling off the suitcase. "Paul!" she protested, laughing. "Put me down. You're going to break your back."

"Don't worry, ma'am. You're no heavier than a bale of cotton."

"Does the parsonage have bars? I married a crazy man."

He loved the way she laughed, with her eyes crinkled at the corners, not worrying about making wrinkles, and that husky, throaty music resounding in the room as if she felt the mirth all the way down to her toes. "You married a man . . ." He stopped. He had almost said "who loves you." Half-heartedly he finished the sentence. "Who is hungry."

"The way to a man's heart?"

"Sometimes."

"Then put me down and we'll have tofu by candlelight. A real wedding dinner." She wasn't aware of how her voice caught on the word or of the wistful look on her face. She didn't know how Paul almost chucked his scruples and carried her to the bed. She never suspected that, at that moment, her bedroom almost became a wedding bower.

Only his eyes betrayed his turmoil. "How about Häagen-Dazs ice cream by candlelight?" he suggested.

"Paul? The Hilton?" Her pleasure was mirrored in her radiant smile.

"Yes. Steak and lobster and potatoes swimming in butter."

"And the glass elevator?"

He nodded. "That, too."

"And afterward a ride in the go-carts?"

"There I draw the line," he said firmly. "It took me three days to get over the last ride."

"You're in luck, mister. I give a first-rate massage." She held up her hands. "Magic fingers."

Grinning, Paul set her and the suitcase back on

the bed. "Suddenly this thing weighs a ton." He put his hands on his lower back and stretched. "I'm feeling a mighty bad twinge."

"My massages come with a price," she warned him.

"Name it."

"Häagen-Dazs ice cream."

"It's a deal."

They remained in high spirits through the drive to Tupelo, the sinfully rich meal, the trip on the glass elevator, and the ride back home. It was not until Paul had parked the car and they'd walked through the parsonage door that reality hit them. They felt a shyness and a constraint that they'd never before known with each other.

"Well, here we are, Martie." Paul hoped he didn't look as foolish as he sounded.

"I guess you can show me which bedroom will be mine," she said, unable to look at his face. She was afraid he would see how much she wanted *his* bedroom to be hers. How could he help but know? she wondered. She glowed like neon in his presence.

"You can choose," he told her. "Down the hallway there's a spare bedroom next to mine and one across the hall."

"Which one is yours?"

"The one with the purple socks on the floor." He grinned at her. "The last one on the left. I'm afraid there's only one bathroom. It adjoins my bedroom and the one next to it."

For practical purposes—because of the bathroom, she told him—Martie chose the bedroom next to his. What she didn't tell him was that she wanted to be as close to him as possible. Even if there was a wall between them, she thought, maybe she could hear him breathing or moving about or even snoring. She didn't care what she heard as long as it was a sound that connected her to Paul.

He stowed her suitcases in the bedroom, and they made stilted conversation for a while, skirting around each other, tense and nervous, like two people walking on eggs. Insisting that she have first bathroom privileges, Paul paced the floor while she showered. The roar of the water sounded like whiplashes to his overwrought mind. He could imagine each drop of water that touched her smooth skin, and he could picture exactly where it landed. He buried his face in his hands and groaned.

Through a fog he heard her knock at the bathroom door. "I'm finished, Paul. It's all yours now."

The first thing he saw when he stepped into the bathroom was her black silk teddy. It was draped carelessly across the towel bar, a minuscule bit of silk and lace designed to drive him crazy. As if that weren't enough, her fragrance of summer flowers, intensified by the steam, assaulted his already reeling senses. "Lord, help me," he groaned softly as he picked up the black teddy and let the silk caress his fingers. If she had left the teddy behind, what was she wearing to bed? he wondered. Suddenly he recalled his early morning visit to her house and the sheets trailing behind her as she'd met him at the door. She slept in the nude! That perfect body, uncluttered by a single stitch of clothing, was curled beneath the sheets; and only a door separated them. He put his hand on the knob and drew it back. Only a door and his scruples, he amended.

Carefully he hung the silk teddy back on the towel bar and stepped into the shower. The cold water took the heat off the outside of his body, but it did nothing to cool the fires raging inside.

He finished his shower, dressed for bed, and

stood uncertainly in his bedroom. Finally he called through the wall, "Good night, Martie."

"Good night, Paul."

He paced the floor, and she punched her pillow until it was limp. Finally she got out of her bed, and he crawled into his. She stared out the window, and he tossed about until his sheet was so tangled he thought he'd have to cut his way out with scissors. He snapped on his light and tried to read, and she cut hers off and tried to sleep. Finally they both gave up and sat on their separate beds, staring at the wall.

At precisely six o'clock the next morning, Baby stood at the parsonage door, barking to be let in.

Two bleary-eyed people sat up in their beds. Paul hastily donned his pajama bottoms and Martie draped herself with the flowered percale sheet. "I'm coming," both shouted as they rushed out their doors and collided in the hall.

Paul gripped her bare shoulders to keep from knocking her over.

"We forgot to move Baby," Martie said. She looked up at him through her tousled silver hair and thought that if he didn't remove his hands, she would attack him in the hall. That bare chest looked too good to be true, better even than she had imagined in her dreams last night.

"I thought she would move herself. Don't tell me she has a suitcase." He didn't know if his voice sounded that way from lack of sleep or from knowing she was naked under that sheet. His blood pressure shot up to about stroke level.

"No," Martie replied. "But she always sleeps in at night."

"I'll remember that."

His hands still tingled after he removed them from her shoulders. He followed her down the hall, and watching her hips move under that sheet jacked his pressure up still higher. Leaning against the wall for a moment, he took a long, steadying breath.

He needed it. Baby bounded through the door and pounced joyfully on Martie's sheet for a tug-of-war.

"Baby, stop that!" She clutched the top of her sheet as her pet happily ignored her command.

Paul watched, spellbound, as the sheet came unknotted and slowly began to slip down her body. Her breasts emerged, perfect golden-tan mounds with dusky-pink nipples that hardened into tight points as soon as she saw Paul's eyes on her.

Baby gave another tug and the sheet slipped farther down, revealing a golden torso and tiny nipped-in waist. Holding the sheet between her teeth, Baby sat on the floor, her tail thumping softly against the floorboards as she watched the two people standing before her.

Paul and Martie remained motionless in the electrifying stillness, scarcely breathing. If they had been able to read minds, they would have closed the small space between them and melted in each other's arms. Instead they struggled with codes of honor and warped truths, standing riveted to the floor like two kegs of dynamite waiting to explode.

It was her eyes that finally galvanized him into action: they were wide with mute appeal. As lovely, he thought, as dew-kissed pansies. Quickly he crossed to her and caught the edge of the sheet. The blood thundered in his ears as he jerked the fabric out of Baby's teeth and pulled it back up to cover Martie. As his hands touched her bare breasts he had kaleidoscopic impressions of silk and flames and a sweetness almost too much to bear. His hands shook as he retied the knot, and he was certain that he deserved some type of medal for this uncommon act of bravery.

As he bent over the knot Martie fought the waves of passion that threatened to swamp her. She felt as if she were seeing everything through a magnifying glass—the part in his hair, each tiny stubble of his early morning beard, the dark lashes covering his quicksilver eyes. His face was so close that his breath warmed the supersensitive skin along the tops of her breasts, causing them to jut forward under the thin sheet in undisguised desire. She clenched her hands into fists to keep them from pulling his head a fraction of an inch closer. She wanted to cradle his head, nestle it against her hungry flesh. She wanted to feel his lips suckle her breasts, to run her fingers through his night-dark hair and hold him there until the scorching heat inside her burned down to a quiet glow.

Hating nobility and honor and self-denial, she bit her lower lip and tried to focus her attention away from Paul's face. Her eyes wandered down his back. The muscles were tense, bunched and corded under his smooth tan. She was no better off, she decided. Heat, intense as the breath of a volcano, still coursed through her, and she thought she might never be cool again.

"There." Paul straightened up. "That knot should prevent future mishaps."

"Thank you, Paul." Old habits of flamboyance and pizazz came to her aid. "The next time I wrap myself in a sheet, I'll just tap on the wall and let you come in to tie the knot." She commanded her wobbly legs to take her back to her bedroom. "Come, Baby," she called over her shoulder. "You and I need to have a talk."

Paul sank into a chair as she swept grandly down the hall. Lifting his eyes upward, he gave thanks for the small miracle that had kept him from ravishing her on the kitchen floor.

*   *   *

During the next few days they tried to act normal, but under the circumstances it was impossible. Paul went through a private hell every time he went into the summer flower—scented bathroom they shared, and his habit of having his morning coffee without a shirt on drove Martie to abusing her bedroom vanity with frustrated kicks and muttered tirades.

Forced into the marriage for the sake of appearance, they tried to compensate by adopting habits foreign to their natures, seeking desperately to please each other and lighten the burden.

Miss Beulah spotted Paul in Michael's Department Store buying a wild print shirt. "I declare," she later reported to Essie Mae, "you could see that shirt a mile away. It was one of those Hawaiian flowery jobs with big purple parrots and jungle trees all over it. I'm telling you, Essie Mae, there's just no telling what the preacher's wife will have him doing next."

Essie Mae called the Bishops, who called the Rodneys, who called the Grimsleys. Paul was unaware that before he ever reached home his shirt was already the center of a swirling controversy. He unwrapped it, put it on, and went over to Martie's house to surprise her.

She had just finished a Jazzercise class and was bent over, picking up exercise mats.

"Hello, angel."

She looked up, saw him standing in the door, and dropped the mat on her toe. "Paul!" she exclaimed. "I didn't hear you come in." She tried to look somewhere besides that terrible shirt, but she couldn't. It was as out of place on Paul as a neon billboard in a church sanctuary.

"I'm surprised. This shirt is so loud I thought it would announce my presence clear to the other end of the hall." He turned around for her inspection. "What do you think?"

"I think . . ." She stopped and ran her hands over her mouth, trying to make it behave; it kept wanting to burst open with laughter. "I think that if you like it, you should wear it."

"I can't say that I'm overly fond of it." He smiled ruefully down at the purple parrots decorating his chest. "I guess it'll grow on me."

"Lord, I hope not." The truth just popped out. Martie had never been a successful liar.

He grinned at his irrepressible pretend wife. "You don't like the shirt?"

"I think it has its merits," she said carefully.

"Tell me what they are. When I saw this thing in the store I couldn't think of a single merit except that it's the sort of colorful dress you're fond of."

She felt as if a shower of stars had fallen over her, and she sparkled with the wonder of it. "Paul! You did this for me?" She catapulted herself at him and, standing on tiptoe, threw her arms around his neck. Her brain reeled with his intoxicating nearness. He smelled like pipe tobacco and aftershave and November wind. "You bought this outrageous shirt because you thought I would like it?"

As he folded her close to his chest, he decided that he would buy a shirt like this every hour of every day if the result was having her, all sparkling exuberance and soft warmth, in his arms. "Yes," he admitted. "I guess I was trying to show you that I'm not as conventional as I seem. That we really aren't as far apart as you believe." He smiled gently into her upturned face. "And I wanted to please you."

Martie rubbed her face against the garish shirt. "You please me, Paul," she murmured. "More than you'll ever know. You don't have to buy Hawaiian shirts for me. I like you just the way you are."

She could hear the wild thundering of his heart as he tangled his hands in her hair and pressed her head against his chest. "And you please me, Martie. Just the way you are."

They stood for a long while, holding each other and wondering how something that felt so right had become a forbidden pleasure. At last he pushed her gently from him. "Have you finished your Jazzercise classes for the day?" he asked.

"Yes."

"Then get your sweater and I'll walk you home."

"I didn't bring one. It was warm when I left the parsonage."

"In that case . . ." He scooped her into his arms. "I'll keep you warm."

She laughed as he carried her outside and kicked the door shut behind them.

"Did anybody ever tell you that you make a wonderful sweater?" she asked, squeezing her arms around him and burying her face in his neck.

"Maybe I should give up preaching and go into this line of work full-time."

"As long as I'm your only customer. I think a wife should have exclusive rights to a discovery like this." She was so enamored of her current mode of transportation that she didn't notice how naturally she had spoken of her new title.

But Paul did. Her words pleased him so much that he couldn't stop smiling. He smiled through dinner, through the late night television news, and into the wee hours of the morning.

Martie looked at the chicken thawing in the kitchen sink and tried to be optimistic. Look at it this way, she told herself, she would try anything once. Heck, she might even enjoy frying chicken. It was the least she could do after that disastrous luncheon with the district ministers and their wives. How was she to know that preachers' wives are supposed to be seen and not heard? She had merely said that she thought God would want all His servants to have dryers that worked and that replacing defunct dryers should be a simple matter since appliances are furnished with the parsonage. The stunned silence that had met her remark was nowhere near as bad as the private lecture she'd been treated to later by a well-meaning old pro in the business. Reverend Clarke's wife had told her that sweaters with beads and feathers, not to mention gaudy turquoise jewelry, were detrimental to Paul's career. She had further said that ministers' wives should strive to be discreet and demure.

Martie picked up a butcher's knife and attacked the chicken with unnecessary vigor. Maybe she had gone a little too far with Mrs. Clarke, but dammit, she fumed, Paul was a wonderful minister! It shouldn't matter whether she wore beads and spangles or sackcloth and ashes. And she had told Mrs. Clarke so. Thank goodness Paul had not been there to hear it. He'd already gone to his afternoon session.

She glanced at the clock on the wall. He should be home in another hour. By that time she would have a plate of golden fried chicken to smooth over the disappointment he must be feeling because of her. He was probably sitting in his meeting right this minute trying to think of a graceful way out of his five-day-old marriage. She gave the chicken a vicious whack. Of course, that was the only thing they could do—think of a way out of this mess— but why did the thought make her so mad?

"I'll tell you why," she said to the thoroughly mutilated chicken on the cutting board. "Because I love the man, dammit, and I'm tired of being on parade like a horse at an auction. I'm tired of being subject to everybody's approval. I just want to be myself without being tagged and labeled and judged simply because I'm the minister's wife." She picked up a handful of slick meat and sighed. "I thought you had drumsticks. Where are they?"

By the time she was ready to put the chicken in the hot oil, she had talked to it so much that she felt as if she were parting with a friend. "Why don't you come with instructions?" she asked as her flour coating floated off the chicken and swirled around the top of the pot. "Oh, well, all that crust is fattening, anyway."

While the chicken was frying she attacked the mountain of dishes she had dirtied in preparing Paul's surprise. She decided that the parsonage kitchen looked as if fifteen chefs had used it to prepare a banquet for two hundred. But she didn't mind; it was a small sacrifice to make for her beloved. She could hardly wait to see his face when he saw that platter of golden fried chicken.

"I'm home."

Martie whirled around, slinging suds across the kitchen and causing a small whirlwind of flour to rise from her apron. "Paul!" she cried. "You're early. I didn't expect you for another twenty minutes."

Paul gazed longingly at her through the fog of flour. He wanted to kiss the flour off the tip of her nose and smooth the damp curls off her forehead. He wanted to cup her flour-sprinkled cheeks and devour that smiling mouth. But he didn't do any of those things. Instead, he leaned against the door frame and hid his feelings behind light banter. "The Pillsbury Doughboy, I presume?"

She crossed the kitchen and took one of his hands. "Close your eyes while I lead you into the parlor. I don't want you to see the surprise."

He laughed. "I'll just pretend I don't smell anything frying." He took her small sudsy hand in his and allowed himself to be led to the sofa. Still holding her hand, he opened his eyes. "I'm an expert dish washer. Are you sure you don't want some help in there?" he asked.

Martie shook her head. "It would spoil the surprise."

"What have I done to deserve this?"

"It's not what you've done: it's what I've done."

"If you're referring to the luncheon today, forget it. You did nothing wrong." His fingers massaged the soapsuds on her hands. "I've never believed women should be muzzled."

"But preachers' wives . . ."

"Preachers' wives or otherwise," he said, his face almost grim. Martie suspected that some of his colleagues had given him a hard time about her, and her eyes grew troubled. Seeing her concern, his face softened. "But I'm pleased about the surprise, angel. I can hardly wait."

"Ten minutes, Paul," she promised, and practically skipped out of the room.

She did a little jig at the kitchen sink and hummed as she washed dishes. Suddenly she saw smoke coming from the chicken pot. "Good grief! I forgot all about you!" she cried.

Grabbing a long-handled fork, she lifted the charred remains of the chicken from the hot oil. "Oh, no!" she wailed, staring at the funeral pyre of chicken in defeat. "Why couldn't you be golden and beautiful? I wanted you to be wonderful for Paul. Why couldn't you?" Resolutely, she pushed defeat aside and marched to the refrigerator. Taking out a carton of sour cream and a bunch of parsley, she returned to the chicken and began work. When she had finished, she decided that it was a masterpiece of camouflage.

Paul had to bite the inside of his mouth to keep from laughing when he saw her surprise. He knew that it had started out as fried chicken, though what it was now only Martie knew. He watched her lean over and light the candles on the small table. She did everything with such zest! He hadn't known it was possible to love a woman as much as he loved her. He had racked his brain for a way to make this marriage real, but so far he had come up empty. If he didn't get a breakthrough soon, there wouldn't be a shred of carpet left on his bedroom floor: he had paced the poor thing to death.

Martie turned off the lights and looked at him across the glow of candles. "Surprise, Paul! Fried chicken with a new twist."

"You didn't have to do all this for me," he said, smiling. He saw the burned skin peeping through the sour cream and parsley, and he dreaded taking his first bite. He would eat it and grin if the effort killed him, he decided. Not for all the tea in China would he disappoint her.

He put the first bite into his mouth and almost choked. "Hmmm." He shuffled the chicken from one side of his mouth to the other, trying to get up enough courage to swallow. "Mf's mfrrent," he mumbled as the bite finally went down.

"What did you say?"

He took a hasty sip of tea. "It's different."

"Good." She beamed at him. "I thought it would be. I know how you love fried chicken, so I thought, What would be a better way to please Paul than to make his favorite dish? It's to sort of make up for the luncheon. Oh, I know you said it didn't make any difference, but I don't want to complicate your life any more than I already have." She put a bite of chicken into her mouth.

Paul reached for her hand across the table. "Martie . . ."

"Paul," she wailed. "It's awful! Why didn't you tell me this chicken is awful?" She raised stricken eyes to his face.

"It's really not all that bad," he said gently. "It'll just take a little getting used to."

A tear trembled briefly on her eyelashes, then rolled down her cheek. "I wanted it to be wonderful." Another tear spilled over, and another, until her cheeks were wet with crying.

Paul went to her in such haste that his chair toppled over. He pulled her up into his arms and cradled her head on his chest. "It was wonderful, angel. The thought was wonderful and . . ." He stopped before he said, "I love you for it." Instead, he said, "And I appreciate it."

"You're just . . . saying that . . . to make me feel . . . better." The words came out between sniffles, and the tears rained, unchecked, onto the front of his shirt.

Every sob was like a knife plunging straight into his heart. He would have walked on nails rather than see her hurt by anything. Pressing his face into her hair and murmuring soothing sounds, he lifted her and carried her to the sofa.

She curled into a ball against his chest and cried until the sobs became hiccups. She cried for the burned chicken and the sweater with feathers and the broken parsonage dryer. She cried over the Hawaiian shirt and the shared bath and the separate bedrooms. Most of all she cried over a love unspoken and a marriage not real.

When the sobs had stopped, Paul gently brushed her hair back from her face. "Better now?" he asked.

She nodded and hiccupped.

He bent and placed a tender kiss on her forehead. "We'll get through this together, angel. I promise."

* * *

The promise was still echoing in Martie's mind the next night as she sat on the front pew of Faith Church and waited for Paul to come out of his study and begin the prayer meeting. She would be glad when he came out. Her favorite piece of jewelry, a clunky, hand-crafted brass-and-copper necklace, had attracted so much attention that she was beginning to feel like a mannequin in a department store window.

Her heart leapt when Paul entered the sanctuary, and she reflected that each time she saw him was just like the first. He had the impact of a dynamite explosion, and she wondered anew how she had been able to live in the parsonage for nearly a week without giving in to the desire that swamped her every time he walked into a room. She stirred restlessly on the hard bench and tried to elevate her thoughts to more appropriate topics.

Paul's smile was like a balm over the congregation. "I thought I would be rather informal tonight and conduct the Bible study from here." Shunning the pulpit, he stood near the front pew. "I want my new wife to feel very much at home in this church, and I know that you will support her as I do." He reached down and squeezed Martie's hand. "And now, let us begin."

Paul's guidance was so inspiring, Martie thought, that it brought tears to her eyes. The small group of parishioners were moved and involved and participated eagerly. As Paul was concluding the study group, Baby streaked through the door, ducked under a pew, and ran through Miss Beulah's legs.

"Somebody catch that dog," cried a member of the congregation.

Baby leaped over Jolene's feet, dived around the pew, and ran straight up the middle of the aisle.

"What's that in his mouth?"

"It looks like . . ."

The naughty pet trotted around the nave waving Paul's shorts—the pair with bright red hearts, of course.

Martie gasped. "Oh, dear," she said aloud without thinking, "Baby's got your shorts, Paul."

Paul tried to rescue his shorts and Baby decided to play tug-of-war. By the time he had pulled them out of her grip, everybody at the prayer meeting had gotten a good view of the telltale red hearts. Hastily he stuffed the gaudy shorts into his coat pocket. "It seems," he said smoothly, "that our dog has no respect for proper conclusions to our Bible study group." He smiled broadly, and the Faith Church emptied quickly. Everybody wanted to congregate outside and swap versions of the story.

Paul and Martie, with Baby between them, stood in the empty church and looked at each other.

"What are we going to do?" Martie asked.

"I don't know about you, but I'm going to laugh."

She joined him, and they laughed until Baby grew tired of all the hilarity and pranced off to scare up another adventure.

Outside, the story grew and grew until it had assumed an importance out of all reason. The consensus of those who remained behind to talk, those sage minds who ought to know because they thoroughly discussed everything of significance that happened in Pontotoc, was that the preacher's wife was converting him to her scandalous ways, and not even the sanctuary was safe from her influence.

The day after the incident of the valentine

shorts, Martie watched the rain wash against the parsonage windows and thought that things couldn't get more complicated. She was wrong.

She saw the van pull into the parsonage yard, its tailpipe dragging and its painted rainbows peeling. Yelping with joy, she ran through the house, out the door, and into Booty Matthews's outstretched arms.

"Booty!" she cried ecstatically. "Where did you come from?" Ignoring the rain, she clung to his arm and gazed into his dear, grizzled face.

"Hi, sugar." He flashed her a smile that showed his two gold molars. "Got your note. My heart's done broke plumb in two about missin' your weddin', but I said, Shoot, me and the boys will mosey on up there and see what this bridegroom's like. So here we are."

"We?" asked Martie.

"The band. Come on out, boys," he called.

A bass player, the fiddler, the pianist, and the drummer all piled out of the van. "Don't just stand there gawkin', boys," Booty told them. "Get your gear and get in out of the rain." Holding Martie's arm, Booty sprinted for the parsonage. The musicians, with their assortment of fiddles and drums and suitcases, followed close behind.

Seeing them again brought back all the excitement of the road tours, and Martie completely forgot to wonder about the suitcases piled among the musical instruments. She dispensed hugs all around and clapped her hands with glee. "Are you still playing 'Jambalaya'?" she asked.

"Shoot, that's still our specialty," Booty said. "Crank it up, boys."

"It hasn't been the same without you, Martie," the bass player told her.

"I've missed you, too, Rod. Give me that intro

again." Martie tapped her feet to the beat of the music and started to sing.

An hour passed, and then two as the old friends laughed and sang and swapped stories of their exploits. The rain stopped, the sun came out, and Miss Beulah passed down the street, walking Falina Theona. Hearing the music, she stopped. "As I live and breathe," she informed her Persian cat, "they're having a hoedown in the parsonage." She scooped Falina Theona up in her arms and hurried home to call Essie Mae.

Paul heard the music the minute he entered the driveway. Smiling, he parked the car and bounded inside to see what wonderful surprise Martie had for him this time.

When Martie saw him come through the door, she stopped singing right in the middle of "Kawliga" and yelled, "Hey, everybody! Meet Reverend Paul Donovan."

The fiddle twanged to a stop as Paul supplied the rest of the information. "Martie's husband." He shook hands all around and, seeing the suitcases, made a discreet inquiry. "You're here for a nice long visit?"

"Overnight," Booty told him. "We're headed for a gig up near Memphis."

"We're a small town," Paul said, "but we have very good accommodations. The Pontotoc Inn—"

"Shoot," Booty interrupted. "We didn't come all the way from El Paso to stay at no inn. We're bunking with Martie."

Martie's eyes widened as she thought frantically. Her own house was sparsely furnished, and had only two beds. That left three people to share the two guest bedrooms at the parsonage. And that meant . . .

"That's great," Paul said. "We're always delighted to have guests." His eyes met Martie's over the heads of their unexpected guests. If looks could have started a fire, the parsonage would have gone up in flames. For tonight, at least, it seemed the wall between them would come tumbling down, and both were having the same vision.

It was well past midnight when the band was finally tucked away. Paul and Martie faced each other across the double bed in the master bedroom and tried to act naturally.

"You take the bed. I'll sleep in the chair," Paul said.

"I wouldn't dream of such a thing," Martie protested. "It's your bed and those are my friends. I'll curl up with a blanket on the floor."

"Absolutely not. And that's my final word on the subject." Paul spun around and tried to cover his turmoil by taking his pajamas from the bureau drawer. He felt a smothering sensation, as if his heart were expanding right out of his chest. With unaccustomed haste he marched into the bathroom and emerged a few minutes later wearing his pajamas, tops and bottoms. He hoped he didn't suffocate in the things.

Martie was still standing beside the bed when he returned. "Paul, we have a small problem," she said, her mouth so dry she could hardly speak. If fainting had been fashionable, she would have keeled over on the carpet. "I don't own any pajamas. I always sleep in the nude."

Paul already knew that, but hearing her say it made his blood pressure skyrocket. His knuckles turned white as he gripped the back of the chair. "You can use my pajama tops," he offered. With trembling hands he removed the garment and handed it to her.

Their hands touched briefly, and the contact

burned through her, singeing her heart. If she hadn't been so certain that she would be the ruination of his career, she would have pulled him down onto the bed and seduced him. She was fed up with martyrdom, and living under the same roof with the man she loved and not being able to have him was making her crazy.

Taking the pajama tops, she hurried to the bathroom before she did something they would both regret. When she returned, the lights were off and Paul was huddled uncomfortably under the blanket in the chair.

Silently she crawled between the sheets and held herself rigid, trying not to give herself away by restless movements. She lay in the dark, listening to the sound of his breathing, trying to decide if he was asleep or awake. She listened to the tick of the hall clock, the one they had moved from her house, and to the scratching of the oleander bush outside the bedroom window as it was buffeted by the November wind. Sounds that were usually comforting to her grated across her nerves like sandpaper, and she thought she might explode from frustration.

At last she could stand the widening pit of loneliness no longer. "Paul?" she whispered. "Are you asleep?"

"No."

"You know that kiss you gave me? The one that was supposed to last a lifetime?"

"How could I forget!"

"Well, it wore off."

With a strangled cry, Paul shoved his blanket aside and came to the bed. Kneeling on the floor beside her, he gently pushed her hair back from her face. "I'm sorry, angel. I'm so sorry it had to be like this." He gathered her in his arms and pulled her fiercely against his chest.

She clung to him, moving her face against the glorious nakedness of his chest. Neither of them knew when the kiss began; they only knew that the burning thirst welling up inside them had to be quenched.

It was a hungry kiss, full of passion too long denied and dynamite set to explode. It was a time bomb ticking between them, a dangerous weapon that could only be defused by superhuman effort.

When their mouths were love slick and swollen, when the enchantment had provided small relief, when the giant named Desire had taken his tidbit and returned unwillingly to his chains, Paul made that effort. He got onto the bed and lay on top of the covers beside her. Taking her in his arms, he cradled her head against his shoulder. "I'll keep the loneliness away, angel."

"Thank you, Paul." She fell asleep listening to the steady, reassuring beat of his heart.

But for Paul, sleep didn't come. Listening to Martie's quiet breathing and the scratching of the oleander bush, he wrestled the giant all night long.

Nine

Martie held the book up to her face and pretended she didn't hear the conversation on the other side of the stacks. It was impossible not to hear, however, because the voices were crystal clear and the topic of conversation was she.

"Where did Reverend Donovan and his new wife go on a honeymoon?"

"They didn't take one."

"You don't mean to say it! How come?"

"Maybe the poor man just couldn't afford it, what with having to buy her all that fancy jewelry and stuff. Lord, do you notice the way she dresses? Like a peacock."

Martie couldn't stand to hear any more. She shoved the book back onto the stacks and left the library without checking out a single thing. Pulling her sweater around herself against the November chill, she fumed all the way home. How dare they speculate about her honeymoon! Her marriage was torture enough. She just didn't think she could survive a honeymoon with her sanity intact.

Her steps slowed as she neared the parsonage and saw three cars parked in the yard. She hadn't been aware of any meetings scheduled for this afternoon; Paul would have told her if there were. Suddenly a terrible possibility occurred to her. Something had happened to Paul!

She raced over the sidewalk, pounded through the parsonage yard, and burst into the kitchen, breathless.

Paul looked up from a chair beside the table. "You're just in time, Martie," he said, smiling.

She sank weakly into a chair. "Just in time for what?" She really didn't care what she was in time for as long as Paul was all right.

Bob Taylor grinned at her. "Some of us got together and decided that the preacher is working too hard. He's so dedicated that he didn't even take time for a honeymoon."

Was there something in the air? she wondered. Was everybody in town afflicted with the preacher's honeymoon bug? A hundred different emotions rushed over her—joy, excitement, fear, longing, desire, despair. She felt Paul watching her and tried to keep her face from mirroring her feelings. "He certainly is dedicated," she agreed. "He's the most dedicated minister I've ever seen. I'm very proud of him."

"You haven't heard the best part," said Skeeter's dad, who'd been a fan of the preacher's new wife ever since the night of the Halloween festival. Anybody who could get Skeeter as fired up about coming to church as she could was top-notch in his book. He didn't care what anybody else said. "We've contacted a lay speaker to fill the pulpit this Sunday so that you and Reverend Donovan can take a

honeymoon trip. We even got together a little dona-
tion so you can go in style."

Martie couldn't look at Paul. She felt as if she
were on a roller coaster headed toward some
unknown fate. She didn't know which awaited her
at the end of the ride, wonder or despair. She could
only be sure of one thing: with Paul at her side, the
journey would be worth it. "That's great," she managed to say in what she hoped was a properly
enthusiastic tone.

"Didn't I tell you she'd be tickled pink!" the postman said, beaming. "Just like the Reverend was.
Nothing's too good for our Reverend Donovan, I tell
you! We want him to be happy."

"I guess we'll be going, so you two lovebirds can
decide where to spend your belated honeymoon."
Bob Taylor clapped his felt cap on his head and
started for the door. "Jolene likes The Peabody in
Memphis." He winked at Paul. "See you when you
get back."

"Have fun," said Skeeter's dad.

"Don't take any wooden nickels," the postman
added.

Silence descended on the kitchen after the door
had closed behind the well-meaning committee.
Martie inspected the ceiling, the walls, and the
floor, looking everywhere except at Paul.

"Well, what do you think?" he finally asked.

"I don't know. I never have known the meaning
of that phrase."

"What phrase?"

"Don't take any wooden nickels. What does it
mean, Paul?"

"Don't settle for less than the real thing."

"Is that what we did?" she asked quietly.

"There's only one way to find out." He stood up,
solemn-faced, and came around the table. "Pinch
you and see if you're real."

"Paul!" Playfully she ducked out of his way.

He lightly pinched her cheek. "Yep. You're real all right."

"And you're crazy."

Suddenly their eyes locked and the air around them sizzled. Their honeymoon loomed in front of them, unavoidable and awesome.

"What will we do?" she whispered.

"We have to go."

"I know."

"Get separate rooms I suppose," he said, watching her.

Her heart sank. "I suppose." She didn't know what she'd expected. Certainly not a real honeymoon. Theirs was not even a real marriage. And they'd already tried one room—that was too much temptation for anybody to bear.

"With a connecting door," he added.

She didn't know why, but if he hadn't said that, she would have hit him.

The Peabody was a grand old hotel, recently restored, that had seen its heyday during the late thirties when cotton was king in the South. Martie and Paul deposited their luggage in separate bedrooms and began their enforced honeymoon.

There was a knock at the connecting door, and Martie unlocked it to let her husband in. The restraint that had possessed them on their wedding day had returned, making them stilted and almost shy. Behind them the curtained bed took on a mystic quality as it pervaded their minds, spawning rainbow fantasies and impossible dreams.

"I think we're in time to see the parade of ducks in the lobby," Paul told her, his eyes carefully avoiding the bed.

"I've never seen a parade of ducks." Martie was suddenly filled with an urge to pull all their tail feathers out. She had developed this violent streak, she decided, about the time she'd been forced into a celibate marriage with Paul. Sometimes life just wasn't fair, but she would feel better about it if she could pull out a few tail feathers, Miss Beulah's included. "Do they toot horns and play drums?" she asked.

"They make do with a record, a John Philip Sousa march, I think."

"I wonder if they would prefer honky-tonk music?"

"Why don't we ask the ducks?" He took her elbow and together they went down to the lobby. Away from the influence of the curtained bed, they became themselves again, Martie and Paul, two people who lived each day to the hilt.

As the elevator opened and the ducks paraded to the fountain on a red carpet, Martie pointed to the last one, a large drake. "I think I saw that duck down in Mexico once," she commented.

"What was he doing?"

"Drinking champagne out of a silver slipper."

Paul laughed. "That must have been some party."

After the parade of ducks they decided to visit Libertyland. The theme park was still open because the weather, a notorious prankster in the South, was balmy and beautiful, November pretending to be summer.

"I want to ride the roller coaster until I'm dizzy and eat funnel cakes until I'm stuffed," Martie told Paul.

"Roller coasters are on par with go-carts, but for you, I'll make the supreme sacrifice."

She boldly assessed him from head to toe. "You don't look like a sacrifice to me. You look like a big, strapping man who should enjoy the finer things of life."

He scrunched his long legs into the small roller coaster car. "You call this the finer things of life?" he asked doubtfully.

"Certainly. Anything that's fun falls into that category."

"I married a woman who is easy to please."

If the roller coaster hadn't whizzed off on its clackety tracks, the subject of marriage might have gotten a proper hearing. But it fell by the wayside as Paul and Martie clung to their seats and laughed in the sudden breeze that whipped the scarlet ribbon from her hair.

True to her word, Martie ate funnel cakes until Paul observed that she might turn into one herself and become a permanent part of the theme park. They watched the dolphins, listened to a good country band, applauded a sensational honky-tonk pianist, and rode the roller coaster again. Except for the specter of the curtained bed, which kept creeping into their thoughts, they had a wonderful time. Paul was enchanted all over again with the high-spirited child that was so much a part of Martie, and she became more and more obsessed with the generous-hearted man who was forbidden to her.

Hoping to wear themselves out so that they could fall asleep quickly in their separate beds, they returned to The Peabody and dressed to go dancing. Martie soaked in her summer-scented bubble bath, dreaming of the "if onlys," and Paul stood under a cold shower thinking of the "what ifs."

She was still pinning the blue sequined butterfly in her topknot of silver curls when Paul knocked at the adjoining door. She almost dropped the butterfly when she saw him in his tuxedo. "I didn't know you were so gorgeous," she said with a straightforwardness that didn't surprise him at all. "I think you should preach in your tuxedo. Everybody in Pontotoc would come just to look."

"That's an innovative idea. I'll keep it in mind." His eyes roamed over her perfect body, draped in shimmery blue chiffon. "You are lovely, Martie. But then, I always knew that."

As they looked at each other, the air sizzled around them and the bed played its siren song. "Paul," she said softly, "if we don't go dancing now, I'm afraid we never will."

He cleared the huskiness from his throat. "I think you're right." His hand trembled on her waist as he led her from the room, and he was careful not to hold her too tight lest he be tempted to never let go.

The tiny mirrors on the ceiling of the Continental Ballroom sparkled like a million stars.

"Do you like to dance, Paul?" Martie asked as he led her onto the polished dance floor.

"I'd rather watch you." He pulled her into his arms and put his cheek against her soft hair as mood music drifted around them. "But I enjoy doing everything as long as you're a part of it."

The words sang through her, and she wished that she were free to tell him how very much he was loved. She wished that she were suitable and that he were anything but a minister and that all the Miss Beulahs everywhere would drop off the edge of the earth.

They danced without stopping through five consecutive songs; neither of them wanted to let go. Paul welcomed the scorching, searing feeling where her body touched his, and he was thankful that the band preferred dreamy mood music. But even if they had burst into rock and roll, he wouldn't have noticed. He would still have held her precious body close to his, dancing to the slow love song that throbbed in his heart.

He buried his lips in the fragrant hair just above her ear. "I would like to hold you this way forever, angel," he whispered.

"There are no forevers for us, Paul. We both know that." She didn't know how she had the courage to be sensible at a time like this, a time of racing pulse and thundering heart and runaway passion. With the music filling her soul and stars winking from the ceiling, she felt like shouting her love at the top of her lungs. She wanted to drag Paul upstairs to that curtained bed and forget everything except her own needs.

"I'm not so sure of that, Martie. This feels like forever to me." His arms tightened around her, and in that moment he knew he could never let her go. There had to be a way through her barriers. And he was determined to find it.

"I don't want to think about forever, Paul."

"Why?" he asked softly.

"Because it makes me sad."

"Sadness can be abolished."

"Not the sadness of a forever without you." She hadn't meant to say it; it just popped out. She'd had no intention of keeping him trapped in this marriage out of guilt or pity. She sighed against his shoulder. Where was her flamboyance when she needed it?

Paul's feet missed a step at her impulsive revelation. He could almost feel the fence between them come tumbling down. He could almost leap through the barrier and make this marriage real. But not quite. He could still feel her uncertainty, and he would never take advantage of her vulnerability. "It doesn't have to be that way," he replied carefully.

"Tell me why it doesn't have to be that way."

"In cases of the heart, nothing matters except the feelings of the two people involved."

"That's the way it should be, Paul, but is it? Does it work that way in real life or only in fantasy?" She lifted her face to his, and he could see the ceiling stars mirrored in her eyes. "Don't answer that. I want to forget everything and just dance. I want the music to last forever."

"Then I won't let it stop." He could feel the smooth silk of her skin through the filmy chiffon. Her vibrance communicated itself through his fingertips, and unconsciously his hands moved in erotic circles on her back. With the polished glitter of the ballroom around him and the girl of his dreams in his arms, he had a moment of epiphany. This marriage had never been one of appearances: it had always been one of the heart. They had simply been too blind to see.

They danced on, even after the music stopped, prolonging the magic until the lights were dimmed and the band took their instruments and stole away.

"I think they're trying to tell us something, angel."

"You promised not to let the music stop, Paul."

"It hasn't. You're just not listening."

With their arms around each other, they left the darkened ballroom and took the elevator to their rooms. Martie fitted her key to the lock, then turned and said, "Good night, Paul."

"Not yet, Martie." He took her shoulders and lowered his lips to hers, and his kiss was a gentle giving, a reassurance that the music would never stop and that forever was not just a dream.

His strength and confidence wrapped around Martie, and she accepted the kiss as a gift. She basked in its sweetness and felt the glow of it fill her heart.

In spite of his enormous desire, there was no passion in the kiss. It was his way of giving without taking, of showing without pressuring. At last he lifted his head and looked deeply into her eyes. "I love you, Martie," he said with quiet strength. "I always have and I always will."

"Paul?" Though she should have known it, had already suspected it, she was still not prepared for the revelation.

His hands cupped her face and his thumbs traced the line of her jaw. "It's true. I love you and I want our marriage to be real."

"Paul, I can't . . ."

He pressed his thumbs to her lips. "Shh. Don't say anything yet. Let me finish." Closing his eyes, he bent and placed a gentle kiss on her forehead. "I don't want to pressure you or to take unfair advantage, but you must know that I said my wedding vows from the heart. You have always been my wife, and I guess I had to come all the way to Memphis to tell you that."

"I think I'm going to cry. This is even more beautiful than the evening we buried the socks." Tears shimmered on the tips of her eyelashes, and she knew that socks had nothing whatsoever to do with them. She wanted to run and laugh and cry and swing from the oak tree and fall into the marigold bed. She wanted to dance and sing and shout for joy at the top of her voice. The man she loved had just said that he loved her back, and for once in her life she was practically speechless. Her flamboyance had fled and was hiding on the rooftop with the Peabody ducks.

Holding back his smile because he knew her comparison to the sock funeral was meant as a sincere compliment, he brushed the tears from her eyes and kissed the top of her head. "Think about what I said, and when you have come to a decision, let me know."

Her violet eyes were wide and innocent as she

looked up at him. "How will I let you know?" she asked.

"I'm sure you'll think of something. Good night, angel."

She watched until he had disappeared into his room, and then the impact of what he had said hit her full force. She shoved her door open and bounded into her room, charged with restless energy. He loves me, he loves me! she thought as she whirled around. Suddenly she stopped. She hadn't even told him that she loved him, too. She had let him go back to his room without even saying those simple words. Good heavens! What would she do now, and where were Baby and Aristocat when she needed to confide in them? And whatever had happened to the fence that separated them? The minister and the almost honky-tonk girl? Maybe the fence was down in Pontotoc with Miss Beulah and didn't extend up here to Memphis at all. Maybe there was no such thing as fences . . . and she couldn't believe she had ever let them stop her anyway.

She picked up the phone book, flipped to the Yellow Pages, and rapidly scanned the column for an all-night florist. Finally she located one in the Baptist Hospital complex and had the hotel connect her. After she placed her order, the astounded florist asked, "Are you sure?"

"Absolutely."

The minutes seemed to drag by as she paced the floor, waiting for the flowers to arrive. At last she heard a knock at her door. She scrambled around in her purse and for a minute thought she was going to have to hock her wedding ring to pay for the gigantic bouquet. When she had finished paying for the flowers, she had three quarters and a dime left, but she was smiling.

She hung the chiffon dress in her closet and

donned her red silk teddy, the one held rather loosely together with scarlet ribbons. Slipping her feet into red high-heeled mules, she lifted the bouquet and walked to the connecting door. Her knock was barely a tap, but instantly the door was flung open.

Paul saw the red shoes, the long, lovely legs, and a bouquet of five dozen red roses that completely covered the top half of Martie. Joy flooded his soul.

"Special delivery," she called from behind the bouquet.

"For me?" By sheer willpower he kept himself from grabbing her, roses and all, and carrying her to the bed.

"Are you the Reverend Paul Donovan?"

"Yes."

"Then these are for you."

"All of them?"

"Yes. The roses and the girl." Martie lowered the bouquet until her shining eyes were peeping over the top. "From Mrs. Donovan with love."

Paul scooped her into his arms, and a trail of roses followed them to the curtained bed. His eyes blazed as he lowered her to the covers, then sat back, savoring every detail of her perfect body. Slowly he reached down and untied the ribbons at her shoulders, watching in fascination as they made scarlet splashes across the tops of her breasts. "I love you, Mrs. Donovan." He lowered his head and pushed the ribbons aside with his lips.

Martie wound her arms around his bare back as his mouth pushed the restraining silk aside. Her breasts peaked and hardened under his questing tongue, and she moaned in response, ablaze with an uncontrollable desire.

His lips pushed the silk teddy farther down as his mouth continued its erotic journey of discovery. "Every inch of you is beautiful," he murmured into her moist, yielding flesh. The blaze burned hotter and brighter, and Martie gasped as volcanic heat ripped through her. His lips and tongue bespoke his love as she plunged closer and closer to the flaming center of the volcano. When she felt its hot breath waiting to consume her, Paul sat back and stripped away the superfluous silk and ribbons. Her teddy settled like a red cloud over his pajama bottoms on the blue carpet.

He covered her body with his, and the volcano erupted. Their love for each other, so long denied, now came pouring out, rich and bright and fulfilling; and they reveled in the wonder of discovery. Behind the gossamer curtains they pledged their wedding vows in a ritual as ancient as time.

When the flame became a soft glow, when their love-hungry bodies were sated and fulfilled, when their hearts slowed to a steady beat, Paul pulled the sheet over them and they slept.

Martie was wide awake. A streak of sunlight peeking through the heavy curtains made a bright line across Paul's cheek. She ran her fingertips lightly over his chin, letting her index finger trace the cleft that she had loved for so long, reveling in the feel of his early morning beard stubble.

He sighed and smiled in his sleep. Martie lowered her head so that her hair swung lightly across his face. He stirred and continued to sleep. Crossing her arms over her breasts, she sat up in bed and contemplated her sleepyhead husband. How could he sleep when the world was outside their door clamoring for them to join the fun and when his early-riser wife was ready for a bawdy romp between the sheets? She swung her legs off the bed and started gathering the forgotten roses. She might as well wake him with pizazz.

Taking an armful of flowers, she slipped through the connecting door and made her preparations. It didn't take her long to locate Booty and the band; he had told her where they would be staying for their Memphis-area gig.

"For you, we'll do anything, sugar," Booty told her when he heard the plan. "Does this preacher husband of yours know what he's in for?"

"No. But after this morning he will. He's going to find out that ours will be a 'combustible' marriage."

"What kind of marriage?"

"Combustible. It's a private joke."

"Right. See you in about twenty minutes, sugar."

"Don't forget the drums," she told him, and cradled the receiver, then picked up the roses and began her preparations.

Booty was five minutes late, but Paul was still sleeping like a rock. Martie belted her terry-cloth robe and ushered the band in. They grinned and winked at each other as they circled the bed with their instruments.

"Okay, boys. Hit it." Booty plucked the strings of his electric guitar, and Martie mounted her makeshift stage and began singing the opening bars of "Help Me Make It Through the Night."

The covers slid down around Paul's naked waist as he shot up in bed. Thinking he was involved in somebody else's dream, he studied the circle of grinning musicians. "What in the world is going on?" he cried—and then he saw his wife. She was standing atop the dressing table, singing into the bristles of a hairbrush. He roared with laughter. "I can see that I'm in for a combustible marriage." Pulling the sheet up higher, he settled back against the pillows to enjoy the song. It took on new meaning as Martie wrapped her husky voice around the words and directed them to her fascinated audience of one. Moving with fluid grace, she took the scarlet ribbon from her hair as she sang. Her eyes never left Paul's as she slowly shook her hair and let it fall into a loose, bright curtain.

At a signal from Booty, the band picked up their instruments and quietly drifted from the room.

The door clicked shut behind them, and Martie unbelted her robe. Paul sucked in his breath as it floated to the floor and she stood before him, naked except for the roses she had used to garland her body.

"Special delivery," she said.

He rose from the bed and walked slowly toward her. Circling her waist, he lifted her from the table. "For me?" he asked, pulling her so close against his chest that only the roses separated them.

"All for you." The music started in her heart and sang through her body as she pressed against her husband, feeling the urgency of his need.

"Then I think I'll start here," he murmured, lowering his head to the garland of roses across her breasts.

Martie's legs went limp as Paul thoroughly appreciated the first floral offering. He carried her to the bed and knelt beside her, whispering, "And then I believe I will go here." She writhed under the complete investigation of the garland circling her hips. "You have roses in the most interesting places," he said, and those were the last words spoken until all the roses had been scattered across the bed and their passion was spent.

Paul picked up a crushed rose and rubbed it lightly across Martie's breasts. "Do you think that fifty years from now you will still be surprising me?" He smiled as her sensitive nipples peaked into tight rosebuds.

"Unless I grow tired of you," she said, and gave him a teasing smile.

"And how long do you think that will take?" Smiling, he tore the petals from the rose and scattered them across her torso.

Martie reached up and brushed a lock of dark hair away from his forehead. "I think it'll take me seventy-five years to tire of your hair." Lightly she traced his lips with her fingertips. "And two thousand years to tire of your lips." Her hands moved down his throat and played across his chest. "Three thousand years here." The hands journeyed downward, stopping to caress strategic points. "Four thousand here . . . and one million here." She heard his sharp intake of breath. "Is that fifty, Paul?" she asked softly.

"Let's go back to one million."

"Here?"

"Yes."

She sat up and pushed him lightly onto his back. Through a thick haze of passion he saw the rose petals fall from her breasts and drift around him. His quicksilver-gray eyes burned across her face, memorizing every line, as she leaned over and fashioned a careful garland of petals. Her hair made a moonbeam curtain on his chest as she lowered her lips to his body and one by one nibbled away the garland of rose petals. She lingered longest over the last petal, taking him into her mouth with it. The carousel music that was Martie surged through him, and when it became a wild, uncontrollable rhythm, he lifted her hips and fitted her over him. The music played on for a million years, or so it seemed, until the carousel wound down to a quiet melody.

"Paul," she murmured into his damp chest.

"Hmm?"

"You're better than a roller coaster ride."

He smiled. "I hope so."

"And do you know what else?"

"Don't tell me there's more?"

"Yes. You're better than fighting bulls and skydiving and doing seventy-five in a forty-mile zone."

"Does that mean you like me?" he asked playfully.

"Enormously, Reverend Donovan."

"In that case, Mrs. Donovan, you can stay."

They ordered room service and spent the rest of the day making wonderful discoveries about each other. Most of those discoveries were made in the bubble bath they shared.

"Paul, I didn't know you had a mole there."

"Come closer, Martie, and I'll show you another one."

"Paul! That's not a mole."

"What is it?"

"I think it's a rose petal."

"You win the prize, angel."

"What is the prize?"

"This." Grinning, he hauled her, bubbles and all, over his rose petal.

When the rose petal had finally wilted and the bubbles had been scattered, Martie rested her head on Paul's wet chest. "I may stay in this tub forever," she sighed.

"That's a splendid idea." He kissed a stray bubble from the top of her head. "It's a great place to learn everything there is to know about my remarkable wife."

"There are some things that bubbles and rose petals don't convey." She lifted her head so that she could look directly into his eyes.

Seeing the serious look on her face, he stroked her back and asked gently, "What don't they convey, angel?"

"Last year I wrote a book."

"I think that's wonderful. Why the serious face?"

"It's an exercise book, Paul, and I posed for the illustrations."

"In that fetching little outfit you call a leotard?"

"Yes," she replied hesitantly.

He smiled and squeezed her tight. "I don't know anybody else who could pose better than you."

"You're not upset?"

"No," he said, caressing her. "Should I be?"

"I just thought . . ." Her voice trailed off, and she let her hands slide dreamily across his chest.

"You just thought what?"

"It's hard to think when that rose petal keeps doing that." Her hands drifted under water to capture the object under discussion. "With you being a minister . . . the leotard is skimpy . . . the pictures aren't exactly . . ." Her breath caught in her throat as Paul shifted to join them once more. "What will people think?" she managed to murmur.

"There's nobody in this tub except you and me. And I think you're splendid. Unless you want to invite an audience?" The question went begging as the Reverend and Mrs. Donovan became totally immersed in their quest for remarkable discoveries.

Finally they were driven from the tub by the fear that they would shrivel away to nothing. They sat in the middle of their curtained bed, and Paul recited love poems to Martie as he towel-dried her hair.

"How did you memorize all that poetry, Paul?" she asked admiringly.

"Terror."

"You're kidding. You're not afraid of anything."

He smiled. "You didn't know my seventh-grade English teacher."

"I wish I could thank her." She leaned her head

forward as Paul massaged the soft curls at the nape
of her neck. "Hmm, that feels great. You're rather
useful as a hair dryer, Reverend Donovan. I think
I'll keep you."

He tossed the towel across a chair and pulled her
into his arms. "And I think I'll keep you."

"Even after my sensational exercise book hits
the stands?" she asked playfully. As she smoothed
his tousled hair off his forehead, she had no
doubts about her husband. He was a forever kind
of man, and she was the luckiest woman in the
world.

"Longer than that," he replied.

"How long?"

He smiled. "Long enough for you to patch all my
shorts." He kissed the tip of her nose. "And deck
my fence with roses." He kissed her eyelids. "And
teach me how to score ninety-six on a par thirty-
seven putt-putt golf course." His lips seared down
her cheek and captured her mouth. "And long
enough to have all my children," he murmured
into the honeyed warmth that was now his for the
taking. He thought his heart would burst with joy.

"That's a long time, Paul," she said when he
came up for air.

"It's forever, angel."

There was no more talking as the shadows
played in changing patterns over the honeymoon
suite at The Peabody.

While Martie took a late afternoon nap, Paul
arranged a surprise. He went about his preparations whistling and wondering why he had been
singled out for all this happiness.

Finally Martie awakened, refreshed and smiling.
"I'm so hungry I could eat the curtain around this
bed," were the first words out of her mouth.

"That's not a bad idea," Paul said, laughing. "And cheap, too. I'll call down for catsup. Or would you prefer mustard?"

"Both. With a side dish of lobster."

"How about black-bottom pie oozing with chocolate and whipped cream?"

"You're making me crazy." She hopped out of bed and headed for the bath. "I haven't eaten enough to keep a bird alive today."

He leaned against the door frame and watched her draw a bath. "As I recall, madam, you had other things on your mind."

"So did you."

"I'm getting ideas right now."

She marched across the tiles and firmly closed the door in his face. "Not until after I eat," she called through the door.

When she emerged from the bathroom, scrubbed and shining, Paul was initiated into the joys of fastening a woman's back zipper. That small chore took ten minutes because he kept stopping to lower the zipper and kiss the smooth skin underneath.

"Paul, that's the fifteenth time," Martie finally protested.

"Are you counting?"

"Yes. You're dealing with a starving woman."

"Is there no romance in your soul?"

"I'll tell you after dinner."

"Then put your shoes on, angel. I know just the place."

Paul made her close her eyes as the elevator whisked them to the roof of The Peabody. "Give me your hand, angel—and don't peek."

"I don't hear any dishes rattling," she said as they stepped off the elevator. "I don't even smell food."

"You will." He led her to the center of the roof,

where a wrought-iron table had been set for two. Candles flickered on the white linen cloth, and a smiling waiter stood beside a serving cart waiting for Paul's signal to uncover the steaming lobster. "You can open your eyes now."

Her eyes sparkled as she viewed the private paradise he had created. Twinkling Christmas lights festooned the rooftop, and a hundred heart-shaped mylar balloons, each proclaiming, "I love you," floated above them. "Balloons!" she cried in delight. "Paul, I adore balloons."

He untied one of the rainbow-colored balloons and tenderly secured it to her wrist. "I'm going to fill your life with balloons and Christmas lights and music."

Her arms wrapped around his neck. "You already have," she murmured.

At a signal from Paul, the waiter punched the start button on a tape player and strains of "Stardust" filled the air.

"May I have this dance, Mrs. Donovan?"

"Now and forever, Reverend Donovan."

As they waltzed around the roof, the balloon on her wrist came untied and floated upward toward the stars.

Ten

The magic of their honeymoon was still with them when they returned to Pontotoc. Paul scooped her into his arms and carried her over the parsonage threshold.

"Welcome home, Mrs. Donovan." Still holding her in his arms, he bent his head and gave her a very thorough welcome-home kiss. "I wanted to do that the first time you entered this parsonage as my wife."

"Why didn't you?" she asked.

"Foolish scruples."

"I'm glad all that's behind us, Paul." She peppered his face with nibbling kisses. "Reverend Donovan, did anybody ever tell you that you're good enough to eat?"

"Did anybody ever tell you that you have the appetite of a truck driver?"

"We've been home only two minutes and already you're becoming a mundane old married man. Not an ounce of romance in your soul." Playfully she nipped his ear.

"I take that as a challenge, madam." With long strides he carried her to his bedroom and kicked the door shut behind them. "I'll show you romance," he said, and lowered her to the bed.

"How about Christmas lights and music?" she asked as he undid the buttons on her blouse.

"This is a package deal." He lowered his mouth to the nipples pouting against her black lace teddy, and there were no more words as the Reverend Paul Donovan properly welcomed his wife home.

After the lights had stopped spinning and the music had become a quiet melody in their hearts, Martie ran her fingertips lightly across his bare chest. "Does this mean I get to move into your bedroom?" she teased.

He propped his hands behind his head and smiled lazily at her. "I'll think about it."

"If your answer is no, I could always rejoin Booty and the band or take up bullfighting again." Her eyes sparkled with mirth, and she thought she had never been as happy as she was at that moment. She was married to the man she loved, and nothing would ever keep them apart again. Never one to dwell on the past, she didn't think about the gossip and public opinion that had parted them once before; she looked ahead, counting all the ties that bound them together.

His arms snaked out and pinned her roughly against his chest. "Do you know how many nights I've wanted to kick down that wall that stood between us?"

"Do you know how many nights I lay awake in my bed hoping you would?" she replied softly.

He crushed her to his chest and buried his face in her hair. "Now that I have you, angel, nothing will ever come between us again," he vowed.

A loud pounding on the parsonage door sent Paul scrambling for his pants. "Stay here, Martie. I'll see who it is." Hastily he donned his shirt and shoes and left his wife among the tumbled bedcovers.

Martie heard the door slam, heard the deep rumble of Paul's voice as he welcomed their guest. She smiled. Bending over the edge of the bed, she picked up her lace teddy and twirled it around her fingers. "I'm just a girl . . . la, da, dee, da. . . ." She sang and hummed and whistled as she dressed, stopping every now and then to stretch her arms over her head like a contented cat. Suddenly she stiffened.

"A dis-*grace!*"

The voice was unmistakably Miss Beulah's. Martie stood very still in the middle of the room, angry color flooding her cheeks as she caught snatches of Miss Beulah's tirade. "Posing half-naked . . . an embarrassment to the entire community . . ."

Her first impulse was to rush down the hall and confront the indignant woman, but then she heard Paul's voice, quiet and reassuring. She couldn't hear his words, but she knew that he would be trying to make the best of a bad situation. She stopped her headlong rush to the door and finished dressing. There was no point in making things any more difficult for him than they already were.

Martie paced the floor as the conversation in the kitchen droned on and on. Portions of Miss Beulah's angry conversation punctuated her restless march in the room that had recently been a little bit of heaven: ". . . it's shameful . . . a minister's wife . . . exercise book, my eye!" Finally she could stand to hear no more. Slamming the bedroom door shut, she covered her ears. It just wasn't fair, she thought. Why did her exercise book have to come out now? That had to be what Miss Beulah was ranting about. *Jazz Your Way to a Perfect 10*, complete with the Reverend Donovan's new wife in scanty attire. She wished she could turn back time and undo that damned book. A year ago she'd never dreamed that she would be married to a minister and that Miss Beulah would be using her book to crucify him.

She balled her hands into fists and swatted them helplessly into the air. When she had told Paul about the book, she had anticipated the controversy it would create; she just hadn't realized it would be this soon. It had been so long since she'd written the book and she'd been so involved with Paul that the publication date had completely slipped her mind.

The gray carpet, already worn threadbare from Paul's pacing since his marriage, took an additional beating as Martie waited for the conversation in the kitchen to come to an end. At last she heard the door slam, then the squeal of tires as Miss Beulah screeched out of the parsonage driveway. Martie raced down the hall and stopped just inside the door. Paul was sitting quietly at the table thumbing through her book. She saw the mixture of emotions that crossed his face—admiration, pride, bewilderment, and something almost like anger. "Paul?" she called tentatively.

He looked up, then said, "This must be the book you told me about."

She crossed to the table and sat down opposite him. "Yes. I wrote it while I was still in Texas. Obviously, it's caused quite a furor in Pontotoc."

"A tempest in a teapot." He flipped to page twenty-five. "I'm particularly fond of this picture."

"That's a position I call the hamstring stretch."

"I'm more interested in the way that red leotard fits than in the exercise," he said, smiling.

"Apparently, so was Miss Beulah."

Paul closed the book and walked around the table. He leaned down and pulled Martie into his arms. "There's no need for you to fret about Miss Beulah. From what I can see, this is nothing more than a good exercise book. Miss Beulah will have completely forgotten it in a couple of weeks."

"But Paul, she had no right to stir up trouble for us," Martie protested. "I'm getting more than a little tired of being the brunt of her rumors and innuendos. And I'm going to march right over there and tell her so."

"I understand how you feel, angel, but be patient with her. She'll come around. It takes Miss Beulah a while to accept newcomers. I think she feels a moral obligation to put you through a test before she will accept you as a part of Pontotoc society." He brushed his lips across the top of her hair. "We'll weather this storm together."

"I don't want to be put through tests. I don't want to weather storms." She pulled out of his arms and marched around the kitchen, flailing her arms in the air as she talked. "I don't want to be patient. I want the whole world to let me alone so that I can enjoy my husband." She stalked outside, slamming the door shut behind her. She was so angry that she didn't notice the chill November air or the paintbox western sky or the mockingbird pretending to be a jay. Her mind was turned inward, railing against convention and a fishbowl existence. Miss Beulah had been the cause of this marriage in the first place, and now she was trying to split them apart. She was nothing but an old marriage pooper. Why did she have to run to Paul with her warped opinions and harsh judgments? Why didn't she turn her imagination somewhere else? Why didn't she take up needlepoint or ceramics or bullfighting? Why didn't she plant a turnip patch and leave them alone?

Martie's shoes slapped angrily against the pavement, and she didn't realize how far she had come until she was past the courthouse. Suddenly she felt the chill and wished for a sweater. She wished she had stayed in the warm kitchen with Paul, secure in the circle of his arms, instead of bolting in her typical, impulsive fashion.

She turned back toward the parsonage, and her feet flew down the sidewalk as she ran home to Paul. Her cheeks were wind-whipped and red as winesap apples and she was panting for breath when she burst through the kitchen door. Her eyes swung frantically around the empty room. Paul was not there. He was probably so disgusted with her that he was scouring the country for another parish to serve. He might even be investigating missionary service in the Arctic.

"Paul?" she called.

There was no answer. She made a quick tour of the parlor. Her heart sank at the sight of the empty room. She had half expected him to be watching the evening news. Damn! He was probably already on his way to Iceland or Siberia, winging high in the sky, forgetting that he had ever known a honky-tonk woman named Martie Fleming.

She ran her hand lovingly over the garage sale end table. Did he know that she loved everything about him, even his beat-up furniture? She had to find him. A daily devotional book clattered to the floor as she nearly overturned the end table in her hasty exit from the room. She ran down the hall, calling his name as she went.

Suddenly she stopped, having heard the distinct sound of water running. Paul had not run off to Iceland or Siberia or the Arctic. He was in the shower! She was too happy even to chide herself as she burst through the bathroom door. She was so happy that she didn't think about her clothes or her shoes or the ribbon in her hair.

Smiling joyously, she pushed open the shower door. "Paul!" she cried. "You didn't leave me!" She wrapped her arms around his soapy chest in an exuberant bear hug.

His laugh echoed in the shower. "Why would I do a foolish thing like that?" he asked as he slipped his arms around her waist and rubbed his soapy face against her hair.

"Because I'm impulsive and irrational and totally unsuitable . . . and I can't fry chicken."

"I don't care if you never cook chicken. I just want you to be the crazy, wonderful woman I married." The washcloth slipped from his hand as he pressed her close.

She rubbed her face against his chest, inhaling the fresh, soapy smell of him. A glob of bubbles clung to her cheek as she peered up at him. "You're not disgusted with me?" she asked anxiously.

Tenderly he brushed away the bubbles. "About what?"

"The book."

"There's no reason to be. You wrote an exercise book, and I don't know who would have made a better model for the illustrations. As far as I'm concerned, that's all there is to it." The water continued to rain around them unheeded. The Reverend Donovan didn't find anything at all strange about his wife being in the shower fully dressed. It was just one more in a series of impulsive acts that endeared her to him.

Martie squeezed her husband and planted nibbling kisses all over his wet face and neck. "You are . . . the most . . . wonderful . . . man . . . in . . . Pontotoc."

His hands began to trace lazy circles on her back. "I was hoping for the whole world, but that will have to do," he murmured.

"You're incorrigible."

"And you're wet."

She looked down at herself. "Paul! Why didn't you tell me that I was wearing clothes?"

"And spoil all the fun?" He took the soggy ribbon from her hair and began unbuttoning her blouse.

When she saw the quickening of desire in his eyes, she put her hands on his chest and rubbed dreamy circles as her body began to tingle with anticipation. "Don't you think I should be mad at you for not running after me when I left the house?" she asked softly.

The blouse splatted onto the shower floor, and his breathing grew harsh as he gazed at her breasts, full and firm and heavy with need, nipples hardened into peaks against the minuscule covering of wet lace. "You needed to be alone," he said with difficulty. He reached behind her to unzip her skirt. Wet lace and straining breasts pressed against his pounding heart, and his hands fumbled with the zipper. Her hands reached behind to help him.

Martie lifted her face and looked hard at him as her skirt hit the floor with a heavy thud. She stood very still, almost without breathing, mesmerized by the promise she saw there. "I don't need to be alone anymore, Paul," she whispered.

"Neither do I." In slow motion he slid the straps of her lace teddy down her arms. The erotic friction of his touch was heightened by the water pouring around them and the soap that still clung to his hands.

The teddy fell to the floor, forgotten, as they came

together, their harsh cries of desire drowned out by the sound of the rushing water.

As it turned out, their magic moment in the shower was the calm before the storm. Paul's return to the pulpit was greeted with mixed reactions from his congregation. Jolene, Bob, and Sam sat on one side of the church along with a faithful group of staunch supporters; Miss Beulah and the dissidents sat on the other.

As Paul looked out over his divided congregation, he silently prayed for strength and courage and a healing miracle for his flock.

Martie felt the crackling of tension in the church and knew that she was the cause. It wasn't just her Jazzercise book, she reasoned. It would have been merely a tempest in a teapot, as Paul had said, if it weren't for the other things: her flamboyant clothes, her less-than-conservative ideas, the Halloween pageant. She was a stranger to sadness and guilt, but both now edged their way into her consciousness. Tears filled her heart. Not for herself—she was more angry than hurt over this latest manufactured scandal. No. The tears were for Paul, for the coldness and censure of his beloved flock.

The usual camaraderie was gone as the congregation filed out of the church, tight-lipped, and headed straight for their cars. The faithful few stopped to chat and shake hands. Paul and Martie stood side by side, handling the situation with pasted-on smiles and stiff upper lips. But it took a toll on them.

Later, instead of a Sunday afternoon stroll along tree-lined streets still sporting a touch of autumn gold, they went their separate ways. Paul disappeared into his study, and Martie went to her former home to lose herself in a strenuous Jazzer-cise routine.

As she twisted and cavorted to the frantic rhythm of a popular rock song, she was thankful that they had decided to keep her house with its large studio. The parsonage was barely big enough for her to practice in when she didn't want to get out, and it certainly couldn't accommodate her classes. Sweat trickled down the back of her neck as she threw herself into the routine, trying to block out everything except the music.

Baby and Aristocat sat on the floor watching their mistress, and when the record ended, Martie sat cross-legged on the floor beside her pets. She scratched behind their ears and poured out her troubles to them. "It's not that I've done anything wrong, you understand." Baby thumped her tail to show that she did. "It's just that I'm in trouble again."

She propped her elbows on her knees and cupped her chin in her palms. "What I'd really like to do is go over to Miss Beulah's and crown her with a potted plant. Of course, Paul won't let me. He said that petunias wouldn't become her." She smiled at her attentive retriever. "Isn't he wonder-ful? Always finding the humor in a bad situation. That's just his way of cautioning me to be patient. If I were in his shoes, I would be a bear. I'd growl at the people who were saying nasty things, and I might even claw a few faces. Sometimes I think he's too kind-hearted."

Baby turned doleful eyes to her mistress and gave Martie's hands a sandpaper kiss, a hearty swipe with a wet pink tongue.

Martie mulled over the problem until she could no longer stand to think of unhappy things. Call-ing to her pets, she locked up her house and hurried home. The minute she entered the parsonage door she could smell the fragrant smoke of Paul's pipe. It was coming from the parlor, which meant that he was no longer cloistered in his study. She was filled with such joy at his nearness that she called from the kitchen, "Get ready to part company with your shorts, Paul. I've worked up quite an appetite." She pushed open the parlor door, focusing on the beloved man sitting in a sagging chair. "And it's not for—" A loud cough on her right caused her to turn around. Victor Cranston and other straitlaced members of his committee were lined up against the parlor wall like participants in the Spanish Inquisition. "Food. . . ."

Vividly aware of her scanty leotard and of its effect, that of waving a red flag before a bull, she bounced out of the tense situation in the only way she knew, with pizazz. Purposely not looking at her husband, she turned the full thrust of her performance toward the scowling committee. "I guess the preacher's laundry will have to wait," she announced breezily. "Make yourselves right at home, gentlemen, and please excuse me while I change." At last she pivoted around to face Paul. She couldn't tell whether he was suppressing anger or laughter. "Did you offer our unexpected guests some tea, Paul? They look . . . thirsty."

She heard Victor's enraged bellow the minute she left the room. "She does laundry on Sunday!" Shutting her ears to the rest of the hubbub, she hurried to the bedroom, shucked her leotard, and climbed into the shower. As the water cascaded onto her flushed face, she decided that it would take something more than patience and keeping up appearances to placate these witch hunters.

After the committee had gone, Martie rejoined Paul in the parlor. She stood quietly at the door for a moment, hating the people who had caused the pain she saw on his face. "I'm sorry," she said, moving across the floor to kneel beside his chair. "I didn't mean to make things worse for you."

"You didn't, Martie." His hands cupped her cheeks, and he smiled down at her.

"I think you just told a lie, Reverend Donovan. It's probably the only lie you've ever told in your life." She hoped that banter would lighten the burden he was carrying.

"Well, maybe I did gloss the truth a little," he admitted. "You're wrong about one thing, though."

"What?"

"It's not the first lie I've ever told. When I was ten I vowed I knew nothing of how Mr. Kirkland's cows got into our corn. My brother, Tanner, saw that justice was served, however. He told Papa that I had left the gate down. I got a sound thrashing for that one."

"Thrashing is not what I had in mind for you." She stood up and lowered herself into his lap.

"Just what did you have in mind for me, Mrs. Donovan?"

"This." Tenderly she kissed the tip of his nose. "And this." Her next kiss landed on his cheek. "And this." She lingered longest over his lips.

"Do you know what I think?" he murmured, tracing the slender line of her throat with his forefinger.

"What do you think?" She arched her neck as the finger moved downward, burning a trail to her cleavage.

"You're much better than a thrashing." He lifted her and carried her into the bedroom.

Their lovemaking was fierce, as if their passion could drive away the outside forces that threatened them. Afterward they clung to each other, each taking courage and strength from the other's nearness.

Martie needed that strength the next day when she was confronted by a scandal-sniffing woman at the laundromat. The parsonage dryer was still on the blink, and a light mist had prevented her from using the outside clothesline. She had put her towels into the dryer and was loading her sheets into the washer when a red-faced woman she didn't know approached her.

"Ain't you Rev'rend Donovan's new wife?" The woman shifted her laundry basket from one hip to the other, causing her calico print dress to hike up and reveal her slip.

"Yes." Martie smiled a greeting. "I don't believe I've met you," she said, offering her hand. "I'm Martie."

The woman took careful aim and spat a stream of tobacco juice at the tin wastebasket. "Ain't necessary for you to know me. I seen them pitchures of you. It ain't fittin' and proper for a man of the cloth's wife to display herself like some Jez'bel."

Martie withdrew her hand. She was almost certain that this woman was not one of Paul's parishioners. Was all of Pontotoc condemning her? she wondered. "My husband had nothing to do with the book, and it should in no way reflect on his ministry. As for the pictures, they are not meant to entice. They are simply illustrations of exercises."

"Call 'em what you want. They're the work of the devil. Ain't no preacher gonna overcome what that sinful book done." Without another word she hitched the laundry higher on her hip and left.

Tears of anger and frustration stung Martie's eyes as she hurried through her laundry. She wanted to go after the woman and make her see the

truth. She wanted to run down the streets of
Pontotoc with a bullhorn and shout that nothing
she had done or would ever do could touch Paul's
integrity. "Dammit," she whispered. "You've asked
too much of me, Paul. I can't change what I am,
and I can't wait patiently for these people to deem
me suitable."

Her Thunderbird made a slash of red on the
streets as she barreled home. The spectacle set
already wagging tongues to further activity.

Her first impulse was to pour out the whole story
to Paul, but he was visiting one of his ailing parishioners at the North Mississippi Medical Center.
Upon reflection, she decided she was glad he
wasn't home. He didn't need further evidence that
she was destroying his career.

Martie's conclusion was reinforced everywhere
she went that week. In the library, at the grocery
store, on the sidewalks, people were engaged in
speculation about the impact her Jazzercise book
would have on Paul's career. The consensus was
that he would lose credibility, that he would
never be asked to move to a larger church, and
worst of all, that he would be drummed from the
ministry.

On Saturday evening, one week after the scandal
had erupted, Martie sat with her arms around
Baby's neck, waiting for Paul to come back from a
district meeting. She knew what she must do. As
she saw his car pull into the driveway, she wiped
the tears from her eyes. Then, putting on a brave
smile, she greeted him with a kiss and led him
inside the parsonage. He must not suspect her
plan, for he would never agree.

She had never been one to use subterfuge, but
because she loved so deeply she put on a perform-

ance worthy of an Academy Award. Having made up her mind that leaving Paul was the only way to save his career, she made the most of their last precious night together. The memories had to last a lifetime. Paul never suspected that their passionate lovemaking that night was Martie's way of saying good-bye.

Pleading a headache the next morning—which wasn't exactly a lie, she told herself—Martie stayed behind when Paul left to preach the morning service. As soon as his car was out of sight she began her preparations. "I know I'm right, Baby," she said to her tail-wagging pet. "I love Paul too much to ruin his career. That's his life's work. He loves it. I won't put him in the position of having to choose."

She sat cross-legged on the bed, rationalizing to herself and to Baby and making lopsided stitches on the front of her blue sweater. "We'll go somewhere we've never been. Maybe Alaska. Somewhere that doesn't have marigold beds. We'll go so far away that nothing I do will ever touch Paul again."

She hurried with her work lest she change her mind. Although she usually acted on impulse, she had carefully planned this scenario. She was afraid that if she didn't do it quickly, she would never have the courage to do it at all. Telling her pets that she would be back soon, she donned her shocking costume and headed for Faith Church.

She could hear the dying strains of the offertory as she parked under an oak tree. Her timing was perfect, she thought. Willing herself to smile, she entered the small church.

Paul was the first to see her. He was standing behind the pulpit getting ready to preach his sermon, the sermon he had wrestled with for nearly a week. Everything flew out of his mind except the large scarlet *A* on Martie's sweater. His knuckles turned white as he gripped the pulpit. He could guess her intention, and for the first time since their marriage he was afraid of losing her.

He watched the heads turn, one by one, to gape at the spectacle. He heard the collective gasps, and there was no doubt whatsoever in his mind that everyone in the church knew the import of that damning scarlet *A*. The pulpit was like an anchor in a storm, and he held it in a death grip to keep from running to Martie and stopping her performance. "There's no longer a need," he wanted to tell her, but he saw the stubborn tilt of her chin and knew that she had to have this chance to make her statement in her own way.

For the first time since she had entered the church, Martie looked at Paul, but then she quickly turned her head away. Seeing him almost made her lose sight of what she had to do. Hastily she made her way to the front of the church and turned her back on him. Facing her flabbergasted audience, she scanned their faces, trying to make eye contact with every person who had condemned her.

"Many of you have labeled me unfit." Her voice rang out in the stunned silence. "My actions, past and present, have been laid at my husband's door. Overlooking the wonderful work he does and the generosity of his heart and spirit, you have chosen to threaten his career because of me." She stopped until the murmur from the audience ceased. *You've come this far*, she told herself, *you can go the rest of the way*. "Reverend Paul Donovan is a good man, and he is not responsible for my actions. I am. Today I'm taking all the disgrace upon myself. Because I love him, I'm leaving." Her voice almost broke on the words, but she thrust out her chin and continued bravely, "I hope you will give him a chance to heal the breach I've caused."

Shocked whispers filled the church as Martie started toward the back door. Quiet arguments broke out among members, and Sam cried out boldly for her to stay.

Paul's voice resounded like thunder in the midst of the hubbub. "Martie, wait!" He bounded from the pulpit and caught her arm. "Come with me." His voice was quieter now, but it still carried throughout the church. With his arm around her, he led her back to the pulpit.

Calmly he ripped the scarlet *A* from her sweater. It settled to the carpet like an accusation in full view of the audience. " 'As a man thinketh in his heart, so is he.' " Paul's eyes seemed to pierce into the very souls of his attentive audience. "The measure of a man is what he is inside. The woman who has been stoned, my wife, has a heart filled with love and joy and kindness. I ask that each of you examine your hearts." His arm tightened around Martie. "I have decided that I can no longer effectively serve this parish, and I offer you my resignation." Keeping a tight hold on his wife, he stepped down from the pulpit.

Martie turned to look into his face. "I can't let you do that, Paul," she whispered.

"I already have."

Victor Cranston was the first to speak. "We can't let you do that, Reverend." His face was red with embarrassment, but he plunged boldly on. "I've been one of the ringleaders in this sorry business. I'm afraid we've been too hasty in our judgment. We've been so busy condemning her because she is different that we haven't bothered to look beyond appearances. Today you've made me realize the enormity of my own failing. If your wife will let me, I'm going to make up for some of the grief I've caused." He took the minister's hand. "I hope you'll accept this public apology."

The rest of the penitent parishioners followed suit. Even Miss Beulah, after much fidgeting and rationalizing, came down the aisle. But once having set her mind to this reconciliation, she put her whole spirit into it. Pumping the minister's hand, she beamed at him. "I do vow and declare. Sometimes it takes a downright *tornado* to get some folks to see the light. Your announcement just left me speechless. *Speechless!* Why, we'd be lost without you. And who else would we find who could put away as much fried chicken? Why, the picnics wouldn't seem right a'tall without you. And as I was saying to Essie Mae, the other day . . . Essie Mae, I said, we need to do something nice for that Reverend's cute little new wife. Why, Essie Mae, I said—"

"Beuler!" Essie Mae interrupted the endless flow of words. "Why don't you move over and let somebody else talk a while?"

The laughter broke the tension, and with the crisis finally over, peace was restored to the little redbrick church.

In the quiet of the parsonage, Paul took his wife into his arms. "Would you really have left me?" he asked.

"I don't know, Paul." She pressed her cheek against his chest so that she could hear the steady, reassuring beat of his heart.

"I'm glad I didn't have to find out."

"You'll never have to find out." She grinned impishly up at him. "You're stuck with me now, Reverend Donovan."

"I think this calls for a celebration."

"Häagen-Dazs ice cream?" she asked innocently.

"I had something else in mind, but if you'd prefer ice cream . . ." The sentence trailed off as Martie reached up and removed his clerical collar.

"The ice cream can wait."

Epilogue

Even the newly installed ceiling fan couldn't relieve the torrid heat. Sweat trickled down Martie's bare arm as she reached up to drape the Christmas bells across the parlor door frame. Every now and then she stopped to rest.

Baby and Aristocat paraded grandly through the parlor, stopping long enough to sniff the cedar tree and to stare at themselves in the mirrored ornaments that festooned its branches. Baby soon grew bored with her image, however, and padded across to Martie's sagging chair for her daily quota of petting.

Martie scratched behind her ears. "You'll soon have some competition," she told her pet. "What do you think of that?"

Baby thumped her tail on the polished floor, then blithely left for the flower garden.

The screeching of tires on the gravel driveway caught Martie's attention. She looked out the window and smiled. Miss Beulah, dressed to the hilt in a straining pink-and-blue-striped leotard, squeezed out of her aging Cadillac, bearing gifts in both arms. As she ambled up the walk, the stripes on her leotard undulated like Old Glory in a brisk breeze.

"Yoo-hoo!" she called through the screen door. Without waiting for an answer, she barreled into the parlor, talking with every breath. "Now don't get up, Martie. In your condition you need to rest. Put your feet up on that ottoman. They look a little puffy. The Reverend would have a conniption fit if anything happened to you." She stopped talking long enough to plop down onto the sofa, not even lifting an eyebrow at the Christmas decorations. Everybody in Faith Church now looked on the antics of the preacher's wife with fond tolerance. "Whew! It's hot enough to fry an egg out there. I said to Essie Mae the other day . . ." She clapped a fat hand over her mouth. "Saints preserve us! Listen to me running on like that. I'm such a chatterbox I plumb forgot about the baby gifts."

Martie took the proffered gifts and untied the ribbons. A pink stuffed elephant poked its snout up from one box, and a plush monkey smiled up from the other. "Thank you, Miss Beulah," Martie said enthusiastically. "These are adorable!"

"The elephant is the way I look now, and the monkey is the way I'm going to look if I can get page eighty-six of your Jazzercise book down pat. Just how did you get your legs to do that?"

Miss Beulah stayed for a glass of lemonade and even helped Martie finish hanging the Christmas bells. After she left, Martie thought how good it felt to count Miss Beulah as one of her friends. She put the lemonade glasses into the dishwasher and was still smiling when her husband came through the door.

Joy welled up inside him and spilled over as he swept his wife off her feet and gave her a thorough and proper greeting. "Ummm," he said. "You taste good. What is that flavor?"

"Pink lemonade." She rubbed her cheek against his. "I have a surprise for you, Paul. Take me into the parlor."

"Both of you?" he quipped. "You're getting a mite heavy, angel."

"It's all your fault, Reverend Donovan."

He stopped when he saw the decorations, and a huge grin lit his face. Life with Martie would always be a celebration, he thought. "Christmas in July?"

"Do you like it?"

"I adore it." He bent his head and murmured against her lips, "And I adore you."

"Paul," she said after a long while, "I've always wanted to have a baby during the Christmas season."

"With lots of practice, I think we can make it next time." He left the parlor, passed through the kitchen long enough to lock the door, and strolled down the hall.

Martie observed the entire proceedings from her vantage point in his arms. "Where are we going?" she asked unnecessarily.

"To practice."

Behind them the ceiling fan stirred the branches of the cedar tree and set the mirrored ornaments to tinkling in joyful celebration.

THE EDITOR'S CORNER

We are simply delighted that you enjoyed the peek into the future we gave you by printing the schedule of LOVESWEPT romances in our March books. And, by overwhelming demand, we're giving you the schedule for the rest of the year. But—please!—*don't* write for copies of these books! They aren't printed ... and there is simply no way we can deal with your requests for advance copies or orders. The reason I ran (and am running now) the schedule in advance is to try to answer your questions about which authors are coming up. Okay? So, here is our list for the rest of 1986.

OCTOBER 1986

#159—TOO MANY HUSBANDS
   by *Charlotte Hughes*
#161—SEEING STARS
   by *Fran Baker*

#160—BEDSIDE MANNERS
   by *Barbara Boswell*
#162—SECRETS OF AUTUMN
   by *Joan Elliott Pickart*

NOVEMBER 1986

THIS STELLAR MONTH
IS LOADED WITH
LOVESWEPT SURPRISES,
INCLUDING A UNIQUE
PUBLISHING EVENT
IN SERIES ROMANCE.
BUT YOU'LL HAVE TO
REIN-IN YOUR CURIOSITY
FOR A COUPLE OF MONTHS!
WE'LL GIVE YOU ALL
THE DELICIOUS DETAILS
IN THE AUGUST EDITOR'S CORNER.

(continued)

DECEMBER **1986**

Oh, by the way, the title of Peggy Webb's September LOVESWEPT, #157, was changed from **MONKEY BUSINESS** to **DUPLICITY,** a much more apt title! Under any title, however, you wouldn't want to miss this delightful romance.

Now, a few words about next month's LOVESWEPTs.

Nancy Holder gives you yet another of her marvelously original romances in **ONCE IN LOVE WITH AMY,** LOVESWEPT #147. Set on a transatlantic liner, this delightful romance features Amy van Teiler, to whom you were introduced in **HIS FAIR LADY;** Amy was the heroine's younger sister, remember? Now Amy is all grown-up and off to England to start a new job. On board she meets the devastatingly handsome actor Derek Morgan . . . a true heartbreaker and a true mystery man. There are many things going on during this cruise: a mystery book club's special event, a party of wealthy and eccentric people recreating the voyages of socialites of the 1930s—for which Amy has created all the costumes. But, ladies, you know what they say about shipboard romances . . . and poor Amy's heart just may be in jeopardy because of the dashing Derek.

Next month with **ALWAYS,** LOVESWEPT #148, Iris Johansen gives you the first of another of her "paired" love stories, so I know you'll be watching the secondary characters to determine for yourself whose love story will be told in the spinoff, **EVERLASTING. ALWAYS** is one of Iris's most touching, dramatic romances, ranking right up there in emotional impact on me with **THE LADY AND THE UNICORN** and **THE RELUCTANT LARK.** At long, long last that dear man who watched over Lance and Alex and David and the children gets his own true love. Of course, the hero is Clancy Donahue! And, of course, Iris has created an exceptional lady for him in lovely, spirited, yet haunted Lisa . . . I don't want to give away any of the intricate and fast-moving plot in **ALWAYS,**

(continued)

so I will only tell you that there are tears as well as chuckles in store for you in this wonderful tale.

The heartwarming, offbeat, humorous, utterly enchanting love stories of Kay Hooper always delight us. And none has delighted us here at Bantam more than **TIME AFTER TIME**, LOVESWEPT #149. Alex Bennet is a tiny woman physically, but her heart, soul, and courage are enormous. Noah Thorne is everything that a hero should be ... with a special dimension to his character that makes him truly the match for Alex. She is a former circus lion tamer, now an interior decorator, and Noah is the owner in residence of the building that she is working on. From the moment they meet—under most unusual circumstances—they are swept along in an irresistible tide of emotion. And, I assure you, you will be too as you read this riveting love story.

HOT TAMALES, LOVESWEPT #150, is another total charmer from the pen of that wonderful romance writer Sara Orwig. As sensual as it is funny as it is original, **HOT TAMALES** is the story of a rather uptight heroine, Clarice Jenkins, and a very free-spirited hero, Grady O'Toole. Grady sets up a tamale stand next to Clarice's uncle's rather grand restaurant ... and fireworks start. A totally lovable pair, Clarice and Grady struggle along the rocky road to love, and their journey will warm your heart while setting your funny bone to tingling.

What a quartet of love stories you have to look forward to next month! Enjoy!

Warm good wishes,

Sincerely,

Carolyn Nichols

Carolyn Nichols
   Editor
LOVESWEPT
Bantam Books, Inc.
666 Fifth Avenue
New York, NY 10103

 # LOVESWEPT

Love Stories you'll never forget by authors you'll always remember

☐	21699	**Rachel's Confession #107** Fayrene Preston	$2.25
☐	21716	**A Tough Act to Follow #108** Billie Green	$2.25
☐	21718	**Come As You Are #109** Laurien Berenson	$2.25
☐	21719	**Sunlight's Promise #110** Joan Elliott Pickart	$2.25
☐	21726	**Dear Mitt #111** Sara Orwig	$2.25
☐	21729	**Birds Of A Feather #112** Peggy Web	$2.25
☐	21727	**A Matter of Magic #113** Linda Hampton	$2.25
☐	21728	**Rainbow's Angel #114** Joan Elliott Pickart	$2.25
☐	21730	**Riley In the Morning #115** Sandra Brown	$2.50
☐	21738	**Midnight Ryder #116** Joan Elliott Pickart	$2.50
☐	21732	**Landslide Victory #117** Barbara Boswell	$2.50
☐	21733	**His Fair Lady #118** Nancy Holder	$2.50
☐	21712	**The Stallion Man #119** Joan Bramsch	$2.50
☐	21731	**Before and After #120** Hertha Schulze	$2.50
☐	21734	**Tempest #121** Helen Mittemeyer	$2.50
☐	21735	**A Summer Smile #122** Iris Johansen	$2.50

Prices and availability subject to change without notice.

Buy them at your local bookstore or use this handy coupon for ordering: